Me Ki Gai

A Young Man's Journey Discovering his Ikigai

By Atul Khekade

Edited By: Seun Adesida

What You seek is Seeking you.
—Rumi

"It's not enough to have lived. We should be determined to live for something."
—Winston S. Churchill

Imagination is everything. It is the preview of life's coming attractions.
—Albert Einstein

In the middle of difficulty lies opportunity.
—Albert Einstein

Contents

About The Cover Page:

Artist : *Dragan Bilic*

Book cover was inspired by two concepts. One is of the Ikigai diagram, and the other is the astronomical phenomenon of birth of a star.

Ikigai Diagram

Birth of a star

Stars are born within clouds of dust and scattered throughout most galaxies. Turbulence deep within these clouds gives rise to knots with sufficient mass that the gas and dust can begin to collapse under its own gravitational attraction. As the cloud collapses, the material at the center begins to heat up. Known as a protostar, it is this hot core at the heart of the collapsing cloud that will one day become a star.

Reference : *NASA Science*

Note to Readers:

I've spent a large part of my young-adult life seeking my free flow zone. The more I have tried to discover it, the more I felt I should have started it early. Self-discovery, *Ikigai* along with financial education should be part of formal education very early on. Atleast, I missed it.

I wanted to experiment with the philosophical wisdom of *Ikigai* with fictional imagination that could create a deeper effect into the minds of a reader.

2020 has been a year of change. The year 2020 will re-define how the world economy works. Every industry from Education to travel, pharma to sports, Real estate to entertainment will change.

We are going to need a lot many intra-preneurs and entrepreneurs to turn the economy around. But that can not be done with the same principles of centralised industrialisation that got us here. A better localised, decentralised and enriching economy along with personal lives can be built. Principles of *Ikigai* may greatly help in that.

I wrote the first version manuscript of this book in 2012. For years, It stayed dormant in my cloud folder. The turn of events in 2020 along with an inspiration from *Ikigai* (Hector Garcia, Francesc Miralles) somehow turned this into a book with the help of Seun Adesida.

I hope the readers will find this book effortless to read, yet grasp the principles that Ive tried to simplify.

There is more about me on the second last page of the book and the back cover including my contact info.

I'll be looking forward to your feedback.

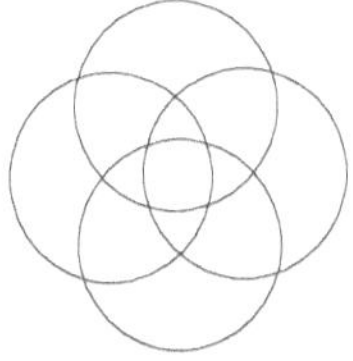

Chapter 1

It was a sunny afternoon in Mumbai. Cars were stuck in traffic and the city wouldn't let anyone slow it down from the hustle and bustle of its urban life. Life in Mumbai had its peculiarities. Apart from being a major economic portal for South, West and Central Asia, it was a city enamoured by wealth and by a high-income elite workforce in finance, industry, commerce, and Bollywood. There was also the prominent presence of slums—a reminder of the burgeoning influx of rural dwellers caught in the daily struggle for a hopeful transition to a more fortunate city life. The city's fuss and the subtle innuendoes of social life, whispered loudly to curious souls that the cure for failure in the city was to be out and about.

Parth, in his early twenties, was pacing towards the skyscraper office complex with dark clouds circling his mind. He had tried so hard to hold back the tears that had now formed in his eyes as he felt the tightening weight and heat of rejection flushing through his chest and face. The despondency he felt from the crumbling elements in his life for two grinding years seemed like it could only get worse. He had felt crippled and confined, but now it felt like his legs were being amputated with a Gigli saw with nothing to kill the pain, and he just couldn't stand the torture anymore. If he couldn't solve his problems, he at least wanted the freedom to end it all.

He got into an elevator and reached the top floor. From there he took the stairs leading to the terrace. It was an eighteen storey building and Parth had managed to dodge the little security posted to safeguard the place. Unlike the newly constructed office complexes with their sensational buzz and earnest security protocols, this fifteen year old building had much less security.

The weight of heaviness caught up with Parth's pace as he slowly inched towards an edge of the terrace and leaned forward to look downwards. It was a scary and horrific view from the top. Parth closed his eyes as he relived graphic images, shocks and events from the last two episodic years of exertion and pain. All the memories of rejection, disappointment, pain, and depression slowly flashed through his mind, making him more certain that this world did not have a place for him, which was why he was saying good-bye to it. As he drew some breath to strengthen his heart and go for the quit, he wanted this to be a free fall and the last whiz of wind he would feel before the final cold smash on the hard ground below.

"Congratulations. You have the job. You will resume officially on Monday after the upcoming training this Thursday and Friday", the manager had said to Parth after he was picked for his first job.

The last couple of years of his life hadn't been inspiring. Parth had financial pressures in his family. His dad was recently retired from government service and the family desperately needed an earning member. His younger brother was still in college and was in his penultimate year. Parth had been classified as a boy with average intelligence due to the average marks he scored to complete his graduation. Upon graduation, Parth started looking for a job that could give his family the much needed financial support.

This period of job search soon turned itself into a test and Parth did everything possible in his commitment to find a solution. After many interviews, he finally landed a job at a technology-based loan company as a telemarketing staff and loan processor. The job required making about a hundred calls per day to convince people to take a loan. It was a profile that Parth hated badly, but he was left with no other option than to continue with the job and the salary it offered every first day of the month. His family needed the money.

Ashwini was the gorgeous girl Parth had fallen for while in college. She was a major toast on campus. Everyone wanted a piece of her and courted her fancy because of her charm, beauty, and brains. Ashwini was sweet, very bright in her academics and had clear career pursuits. These qualities easily earned her the tag "Beauty with brains", and made her such a valuable attraction.

"Hi Parth", Ashwini had greeted, "you look worried, are you fine?"

"I am good Ashwini, just a little stressed? I have had so much to deal with lately. I guess I need a little rest."

"Try to take good care Parth, make this weekend count by trying to catch a good rest."

Parth felt the blush rush to his face, he fought hard to ensure Ashwini didn't see it. His heart felt the warmth well up as he replayed the scene severally in his mind. The kindness in her voice, the tenderness in her eyes, and the sincerity of her words all got him ecstatic. If only she knew how he cared about her, but their conversations never went beyond these greetings, though Parth felt that she seemed to care in a special way.

At first he thought it was because he had been shy and hadn't acted on the cues Ashwini had left him, she seemed to really care about him, or so he thought until he tried to get closer. The closer he tried to get, the more it seemed like she deliberately began to avoid him and to keep things at a formal acquaintance.

"I am just confused. Could Ashwini just be scared of making a commitment? Has someone hurt her before? She seems to want something, at the same time she never gives the allowance. Could she be getting me into a chase? Ashwini, I won't hurt you. Or could it be I am not cool enough for you?" These were the thoughts and questions that bogged Parth's mind in their final year of college.

Parth was getting frustrated as he never seemed to get anything he wanted. His family sagged under financial pressures, his efforts to improve his grades came out abysmal as he seemed too slow for the fast pace of things around him. Now he had been chasing Ashwini for some time but she didn't seem to show the same interest in him—at least she didn't allow things get close enough. She had occasional conversations with him, just as she did with other guys.

It was also clear she had a brighter chance at career than he did. She had emerged from the IT tests as part of the few candidates to be selected to work for MindSys, the best IT Company in the country. She got a handsome package.

Parth only got more attracted to Ashwini.

She was never rude to anyone and was very sociable—only that she had too many guys around her. Her light brown eyes were bright and fitted well into her heart-shaped face. Her hair carried such elegance in its dark, straight and silky texture—it was just the way he loved it, neither too long nor too short. She was fair and slender, and her body well accentuated by moderate curves. He kept thinking of how to get ahead of the pack, but it seemed more herculean to distinguish himself.

Every conversation that he had with her pulled him towards her and made him think more about her—even though many of those conversations were in his mind. Ashwini one day winked at him at a hang-out he had managed to attend. He glided through the crowd, holding her gaze as they met-up and chatted. He said something that made her giggle so heartily that she gave him a peck. He couldn't believe his luck. He savoured the waves of current that coursed through his body until someone bumped into him and shook him out of his reverie—it had all been his fantasy. He felt ashamed and left the party earlier than planned. He wondered if anyone had noticed him ogling at her.

Parth was an introvert and had a very sensitive mind. The attraction kept growing every day, numbing his senses and swirling around his emotions. He was convinced he was in love with Ashwini, and every time he saw a romantic movie of a young hero chasing his love, he felt the adrenaline rush urging him to do the same.

Parth kept imagining how he would scheme and chase the woman of his dreams and turn out victorious in life at last. Soon enough this emotional side of his life became a twist; it was harder than he thought and he didn't want to be forward. What truly started at first as a chase was soon becoming more like a meaningless pursuit.

"Hi!" Parth called out from across an aisle in the grocery store, he could almost swear it had been over a month they last saw each other.

Exams and dissertations had kept many students scarce and buried in work. Ashwini smiled and walked over to say hello. They chatted for a while and exchanged numbers as they walked out of the store together. Parth felt a rejuvenated connection and followed it up with frequent messages. Soon enough, Ashwini wasn't responding to his messages anymore and it only made him anxious and furious. He then decided to call instead whenever he felt the urge to talk to her.

Ashwini was a career focused girl but had the common feminine characteristic of attracting the attention of admirers. Parth was perhaps just another of such guys who fancied her, nothing serious. She was used to it, but couldn't always reply to everybody. Everyone knew she had so much on her plate career wise; she always apologized whenever she later met them at a hang-out or in class. She was just busy.

But Parth seemed too caught-up in the maze and refused to accept things. He felt Ashwini was side-lining his attempts, so he chased her even more. He tactically showed up at places where she could be in order to force a co-incidence and strike conversations. He kept at it.

*   *   *

The media had been awash with reports on how information technology and software applications were transforming the landscape and shaping the future of work. Analysts kept projecting on the millions of new jobs that would be created by the on-going digital revolution.

Securing a job in a software firm, big IT company, or call center agency, was fast dominating the discussions by parents, middle-class families, poor households and youths alike. Undergraduates that looked forward to high paying careers formed the major part of the loop and were enchanted in the fabulous offers companies were making. Companies were flooding campuses to find the best talents for recruitment.

"Can you believe that guy struck a deal for $5,000 per month?" somebody in a small group holding one of those impromptu career conversations had said.

"That's 60 grand of USD per annum! 40 Lakhs per year? I can't believe it!" he exclaimed

"Well I know of another guy who got a Stack Developer job for $8,000." Someone else said.

"He had been working on stuff since year two and he is quite good. These tech companies are spending big, all we need do is get really good and boom!...We begin to fly!"

Another discussant interjected and said "But hey guys we have to be real. Not everyone will get those kinds of jobs because most packages are between 6.5 to 10 Lakhs per annum for freshers. If you have good grades you could get between 10-20 Lakhs. So keep your grades up and try to know your stuff well, particularly if you aren't a genius who could get the 40lakhs kind of job."

Anytime Parth heard such discussions, he didn't know what to make of himself. It was common place to find small groups of students discussing such things, especially when the talent test results were out. Parth was finding it difficult to continue taking the tests that the top technology companies conducted every semester. He had attended about ten of them and while most of his classmates had a campus placement offer, he had not even cleared the first level of tests—which were considered to be at the basic aptitude level.

Parth found it hard to concentrate on a test format where aptitude was measured within only a time span of half an hour. He could hardly understand the questions and by the time he understood them, the test time was over. This was why he avoided discussions about career prospects. Something in him kept shrinking as he ruminated on the possible consequences of his poor test performances on the quality of jobs he could secure. He also thought of how it extended to the quality of life he could afford for himself and that which he could help his family achieve.

After he graduated from college, the daily worry within the family only troubled his soul the more; he desperately needed an income that could help support the family. Parth was raised by a lower middle class family that lived in a 400 sq ft low profile chawl structure where one had to walk a hundred meters to go to the bath and washroom, while they could barely meet their expenses. Parth's parents came from a cultured family and gave good Sanskar and religious teachings to both their kids.

The humble atmosphere in which they were raised did not deter them from dreaming that they would overcome all problems one day and live a very good life. Parth's parents had ensured that their kids attended good schools and had qualitative college education even when paying the fees was quite a burden on their finances. The family had to service loans to support their children's education and it strained them—but they believed the investment was worth it.

"You should join an IT company" said Abhay, Parth's father. "They are paying very good salaries. The job will also take you places all over the world."

Abhay had his ears filled everyday from the daily banter he had with his friends, and some of the testimonies were nothing short of magical. His mouth had actually caught a fly recently when he practically gawked agape at the story of Bablu the shoe cobbler and popular street talkative.

Bablu was easily the best in the area, but you had to sit with him if ever you were going to get your shoe fixed, otherwise you could as well have left it at home because it sure wouldn't get done. The reason was simple, Bablu claimed he was the busiest man in the area and didn't have the time to attend to customers who couldn't wait.

While Bablu held down his customers, he filled them in or got filled in on the latest gossip in town. His spot became the rallying point for the local news served hot. His good looks, strong physique and boastful lips seemed to earn him a good followership. He didn't believe in marriage, he said he was a gift to any woman who had the guts to raise the children while he remained free. Now one of those five children from five different women had become the most sought-after tech gurus in Mumbai and had moved the entire family to a big house in the city.

Abhay kept wondering where they got it wrong with their kids, "Parth doesn't seem enthusiastic about life or big ambitions and I am not quite sure about Tejas", he thought to himself.

That evening, Abhay didn't know if the reason he kept spitting was from the irritation of the big fly that had buzzed into his mouth to take undue advantage of his shock, or if it was the sickening feeling he felt in the pit of his belly as he remembered his sacrifices and what he thought was the irony of life unfolding right before his eyes.

Parth was excited about his father's idea that a tech job would take him to places he had never been—he had always loved traveling, only that while growing they couldn't afford too many trips. What Parth was however half-hearted about was whether he really wanted to work for a technology company. He did not like the way they chose their candidates. He wondered if failing ten consecutive campus tests wasn't a signal that he wasn't cut-out for such jobs. He had his doubts and wasn't sure what he would do. But he knew he needed a job and had to get one. Unfortunately even the non-tech jobs seemed far-fetched and out of reach.

"I'm trying to but I haven't been selected in any" he had responded to his dad's initial statement about joining an IT company.

Subhada, Parth's mother, let out a deep mournful sigh as she listened to her son. "You should study harder", she rejoined.

"Yes mother, but I'm not hundred percent about it, I don't really know if I can do the job."

"How come you cannot do the job? Were you not educated as a technology engineer?"

Parth had his self-belief questioned once again. He always knew at the back of his mind that something was not right about the wave that was unfolding in front of him; from the inside he wanted something different. But anyone that Parth talked to had been able to convince him that there was something lacking in him that he needed to look out for. This had nearly made Parth lose all his self-esteem and his ability to face life. He wasn't sure he could find fulfillment and ever attain his desires for prosperous living.

* * *

Subhash's name came up as the caller I.D. "Hi, Subhash"

"Hello Parth, there is this opening at a small Fintech company and they have asked for referrals of trusted people who haven't got a job yet. I thought you might be interested"

"They are not even taking the placement test. All they'll do is an interview."

"Really? when is it? "

"Tomorrow"

Subhash was working in the college as a placement coordinator, and his job was to ensure all placements open to the college were filled by the college's candidates. The Chairman of the College Board wanted the college to gain recognition for job placements in order to raise the profile of the school. When a request came from the loan processing Fintech company, Subhash had found Parth's name on the list of the few college candidates still without a job. He wanted to know if Parth would like his name among those to be forwarded for the company's interview.

Fastloan.com was a digitally driven loan processing company. On the morning of the interview, Parth dried his tears as he looked into the mirror while knotting his tie and preparing to leave the house for the interview.

Parth was happy about the fact that he did not have to appear for any test and only had an interview.

FastLoan.com was a small financial technology (Fintech) and loan processing company which processed loans for big banks. They had an office in the business district and had a staff of about twenty people, majority of which were telemarketers.

Parth sat tensely outside the cabin of the interview officer as he waited his turn.

Parth had got a hint from Subhash that FastLoan's pay package was an average one, but he still thought the amount was good enough to support his family.

The interviewer was very friendly with Parth. After a brief conversation, Parth was getting hopeful that he would land the job.

"You talk really well. You will fit into sales and marketing", said the Interviewer after he had sufficiently engaged Parth on generic talks about the technology industry, life in the city and life in general.

"Do the training this week and you can start work from Monday."

Parth was excited to go back home and tell his parents about the job. He was happy he could now contribute something to the upkeep of the house.

*   *   *

It was a week into Parth's job and he was doing the daily calls to loan prospects to get willing people to open a loan account with FastLoan.com. The Higher the Loan value, the better it was for the company as they were commission agents.

"Parth, come to my cabin." said Parth's Manager as Parth removed his headset and mic, and went into the cabin of Madhur who was handling the team of twenty telemarketers in Fastloan.com

"From today, your job is to make a hundred calls every day and produce five new loan accounts.

"Five new loan accounts? Isn't that too much?"

"Well that's very normal here."

Parth was tensed as he walked out of that cabin and soon realized it was not going to be easy. He was not enjoying making phone calls to people who were peacefully at home, only to ask them to apply for a loan and hear them bang their phone after some harsh response. That was the case most of the time. It was tough selling debt to people when they didn't walk through your door to ask for it.

*   *   *

Parth was surprised that what started as an excitement a few days ago about being able to take a salary home, was slowly turning into a question mark on whether all this was making any sense. The half-heartedness was making Parth make fewer phone calls every day mostly with only a few positive responses.

If anything, Parth was sure about one thing in his life, he wanted a vibrant career. He dreamt of talking in front of a crowd like successful people do. He dreamt of being important. He was very emotional about doing well at something he really wanted to do.

He knew there was only one way through which he could bring about real change and make a difference, and that was with his work.

He was fascinated with famous cricketers, actors, politicians, singers and the category of people who were occupied most of the time with their work. The poverty that he had seen, the helplessness that he had been through, and the problems of his family, he knew that only his work could change all of that. But all these feelings seemed like seeds in the heart. On the outside, Parth was very scared and constantly lost his self confidence with whatever anyone said to him.

Not being able to do something he enjoyed made his head and heart ache, but the voice of the world around him made him overlook it. He was scared to venture on an uncertain route, and he preferred to stick with what was expected from him. That way he had a better chance to take care of those he cared about and save himself from the pain of seeing them suffer.

Parth was equally concerned about the love of his life. He believed in a future with Ashwini. The chase gave him the feeling that he was going to be emotionally strong if Ashwini accepted his proposal.

Parth had spent a few sleepless nights firming up his plan to finally propose to her.

That morning, his heart throbbed. He was quite restless and decided he was going to let the cat out. He knew enough about Ashwini to figure out where she would be. She had a couple of friends who worked at the university and they hung out every evening at a cafeteria not far from the campus.

He was right. Parth located Ashwini and waited for her to be alone. With adrenalin pumping through his body he stood before her when he got the chance.

"Ashwini, I love you and I want to marry you."

"What?"

"Yes, I'm sure. You're the one."

"Ok…???"

"Ashwini, please say yes and I will feel good. We could be happy for the rest of our lives."

Ashwini by now was uneasy, she felt embarrassed. She hadn't seen this coming and she wondered if she hadn't been careless with possible clues. She didn't like the way in which Parth was handling things, and just wished she could stop him without hurting his feelings.

"Parth, you're a good friend of mine. I appreciate that you feel about me that way but I'm sorry I don't"

"But I feel so much about you. I spend sleepless nights thinking of you."

"I see but that doesn't mean I have to. I appreciate that you have feelings for me but I just don't. Please try to understand."

"But Ashwini why not? I thought…"

Ashwini was now getting irritated and wanted an exit out of the situation.

"Listen Parth, I have to go now. As I said, I don't have any feelings for you and I don't think I ever will. Thank you and Bye."

Parth was exasperated. It was like the world was going to blank out on him. How could he have been so wrong? But he suddenly felt he should hide his irritation. He hurried to where Ashwini was.

"Do you have someone else?"

"I'm sorry?"

"Do you love someone else?"

"Sorry that's personal Parth."

"Then why not? At least tell me why not."

"Parth, please now you're overdoing it."

Ashwini quickly rushed to the cab and rushed home to get rid of hyper Parth.

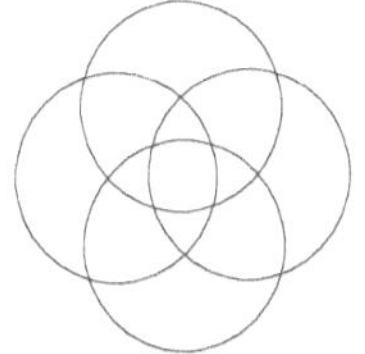

Chapter Two

Parth was now beginning to feel the pressure of his Manager at work. He hated making these calls to people, as much as he hated the curses and swear words. He did not like the targets that his manager gave him, especially because he was under pressure to meet them.

Parth was now hardly doing twenty calls in a day and was frequently absent at his job. His parents were also worried about what was happening with him.

"Why did you not go to work today?"

"Because I don't like it. I don't like calling people when they are asleep or having food to ask them to take a loan."

"But then that's your job, what about your salary? If you don't get it how will you survive? How will we take care of expenses?"

Parth had tears in his eyes when he heard that. He got ready to go to the office. He tried to get another motivation for this tough job.

When Parth arrived at the office, his manager was waiting for him. He called him to the cabin.

"What happened Parth? Ever since I gave you the target, you have been going down. You're hardly making any calls and it's been ten days since you last got any lead."

"I don't know why I'm not able to do it as I thought, but I'm trying my best to."

Madhur was used to the situation. He knew the difficulties of the job and he had handling large numbers of resignations and new interviews every month because of similar frustrations.

Madhur still tried to keep Parth up on the mood.

"Give it another try. Maybe you just need your own unique formula"

"Yes Sir, I will."

Parth felt the burden of work sag him, especially now that his emotional state was very low. He had become really heartbroken when Ashwini said no to his proposal, refused to take any of his calls, and didn't reply any of his texts or emails. She had also blocked him on the social networking platform.

Parth still wanted to have a conversation with Ashwini to convince her of how much he loved her. It didn't work and it depressed him terribly.

At work, he was totally down as well. He did not like what he was asked to do. The only reason he was still on the job was for his paycheck due on the first day of the next Month.

Another week went by and a day came when Parth's life took a sharp turn.

*   *   *

As Parth got up, he had a heavy head and a laden heart. He was a great believer in god and often prayed when he got up in the morning.

"God, turn my life around. Please make good things happen to me now. I can't handle this any-more. Give me the success, love, and happiness that I've been looking for." Tears rolled down his cheeks as he prayed.

Parth got to work early that day holding out his faith. He decided that he would give his job the best shot. He started making calls with renewed zest.

"Sir, I'm calling from FastLoan.com, would you like to apply for a loan?"

"Why are you doing this? Don't you understand? I've told you guys several times to shut the f*** up and never call me again, else I'll report to the police" came the voice from other side who Parth noticed had banged his phone while hanging up.

It was a yet another sad start for the day, even when Parth had woken up early with prayers from the bottom of his heart, asking the almighty to help.

Parth kept calling other prospects and it only got worse. It was half an hour before lunch and Parth's faith had again sunk to the bottom without any success on a lead. A lot more was to unfold.

"Parth, why don't you join me for lunch at the restaurant by the corner of the street?" It was unusual of Madhur to ask Parth to come over with him for lunch.

Parth feeling the weight more on his head, which was banging now with aches inside, shut down his computer and went for lunch with Madhur.

"Parth…I am sorry, but I think you may have lost it. I don't think you fit in here anymore." Madhur was just beginning to open up as they nibbled on what was left of the Pizza they had ordered.

"What? No, I'm trying my best. Give me some more time."

"We've given you enough time. See, it's nothing personal but I feel you should try something else. I thought you were good at talking, but this thing isn't working out well. It was a pleasure to have had you here, but I think you aren't cut out for this kind of stuff."

"No sir please." Parth broke into tears.

A ton of guilt collapsed on him, and overwhelmed him with a sense of failure. The feeling of not being able to do anything meaningful was eating Parth up. He knew that in the light of recent developments where papa and mama had visited the hospital recently for minor health disturbances, going a month without a salary could mean that the family might miss its electricity and phone bills. It could also be difficult to buy ration in the next month. He knew his parents were constantly worrying and it was beginning to take a toll on their health.

"What would I do without this salary?"

"Sir, I'll try my best but please don't fire me. I don't know why it's not working out but I'm trying my best."

"Parth, chill a bit. You're still very young and have a lot to explore. Don't feel it's the end of the road. Something good will happen, but I'm sorry to say it will be your last day here at the office."

Madhur shook hands with Parth as Parth was just about to burst into tears. Madhur turned around and left for the office.

Parth was now really crying loudly. He felt he had let down his parents who had worked so hard and had made many sacrifices to provide a good education and a modest life for Parth and his younger brother. The feeling of getting fired from his first job was too much to take and Parth felt like he was going to have a nervous breakdown.

"How can I stand to see my parents suffer without good health care? They gave up their lives for us."

"No, god can't do this to me after praying out my heart. He should have at least something good for me. He is probably working on something."

Parth tried to console himself and to hold up his mind. His family needed him. He had to be strong for them, but it felt like his mind was about to collapse—he was suffocating.

Everything around him suddenly became dark, he was slipping into depression, and he could feel pricks of pain shoot through his heart as he held the left side of his chest. He took out his cell phone and called Ashwini, he needed her now more than ever. He was hoping that she would talk to him and that somehow her care for him would grow.

"Hello Parth", Ashwini finally answered the call after two attempts. Her voice was like a soothing balm, Parth felt the tightening pain on the left part of his chest ease up, he was starting to feel a little better with just her voice alone.

"Are you there?" Ashwini asked as her question suddenly made Parth regain his alertness.

"How are you? You haven't been answering my calls."

Ashwini was silent from the other end, she expected he would at least be reasonable and show more tact. Their friendship didn't have to end if they couldn't be together as lovers she thought.

"Please talk to me. What do you feel about my proposal? I feel we're made for each other."

"What the hell? Don't you get the message? I told you I don't have any such feelings for you. I'm not interested in you and now I don't even like you. Please never call me again. We're not friends any-more. If you call me again I'll have to ask someone else to handle this."

Parth was shattered. Ashwini had cut the call before he could say anything further.

The world in front of him for which he was trying so hard to work out had shattered him. Parth sunk into depression. His mind blanked out. He felt like he was thrown down from a cliff and didn't know what was happening. He couldn't go home.

"Why am I living in this world if no one wants me? Even god has abandoned me. The day I had confessed my exhaustion in prayer is the day god decides to make the worst day of my life. Maybe he there isn't any god after all. Life is a burden. I am fired from my job. My family will suffer. My heart is broken. I am not supposed to live." He drifted off.

"Hi, are you okay?" Someone had joined him on the park bench where he had dozed off with his head on the arm rest. As he sat up, his side ached, his mouth was bitter and his head felt bigger than his body.

"Yeah, I am fine. I guess am just exhausted. I guess I dozed-off. I guess I would join a bus home now. I guess…sorry thanks."

Parth was now really beginning to have a mental collapse. His pain had become such an ocean of negativity that within minutes he decided that was it. "I am going to quit."

He knew the perfect place where he wouldn't draw any attention. He had visited the historic building severally on excursions while in secondary school.

*　*　*

Parth opened his eyes for the last time before he was going to jump from the terrace of this eighteen storey building. All the memories, the disappointment, the pain was turning itself into a deadly atomic bomb that would take his life.

With one final breath, Parth bent over the railing and closed his eyes again.

"Come back! You don't have to die now." a bold voice reverberated from behind. Parth was long gone, but this voice seemed to break the pipe. He was distracted. He was scared.

A swift strong hand was holding him from behind already. Parth felt a new surge of electricity flow through his body and brain. He suddenly opened his eyes.

"Come back son." This time the voice was reassuring, it didn't have the forceful confidence that had shook his conviction in death.

Parth was exhausted. Fear gripped him. He was confused. He didn't want to die, but he also questioned how he could bear to live. His mind became quiet from fatigue. He still felt wracked by the turn of events in his life, but he was now breathing heavily, and needed rest. He visibly panicked, and all he wanted now was to breathe and allow the traumatic events fade into insignificant memories.

But he really felt quite strange.

"Or did I die?" He thought to himself.

Maybe death was painless after all and he had crossed the line painlessly without realizing.

"Is this heaven or the afterlife?" Why was he feeling as though he was floating and yet so heavy? A strange sensation flowed through his body, he felt like he drifted into another consciousness beyond what he saw around. "Is this heaven? Or the afterlife or what?" he kept wondering.

Parth then realized there was a security guard in white and bright uniform leading him to a corner on the roof so he could sit and regain his bearings.

Parth was afraid word could get out that he attempted suicide and he could even get in trouble with the authorities. He thought to himself "If my family hears of this, what would happen? How could I expose them to that much shame?

"Stop worrying. Just sit back here and rest, you don't look so good."

Parth tilted his back a bit to rest his head. He then looked up with a Cheever on his face but something was strange. Parth had never seen a security guard in a uniform like this before. It was white uniform and it was bright almost as if there was a thousand volt bulb hidden inside somewhere. The face of the security guard which was clean shaven and smiling had a strange aura.

"I'm sorry. I did not mean to do this…I was ….a…"

"It's ok son. Come along let's get to the ground floor", the guard said after Parth had rested a bit.

"You're not going to give me to the police are you?"

"I don't have to. You're a beautiful person on the inside. Besides, you have a great life ahead of you. I'm sure your worries will be gone soon. The only things that you needed to kill were your tensions, your ego, and the noise. You've done that now. You are in your best state right now."

Parth seemed puzzled with this dialogue. This was an over-matured conversation coming from someone like a security guard. The talk seemed very philosophical but Parth was so puzzled and blank that he was just fascinated listening to the voice of this complete stranger.

"Do you work here?"

"Yes, I'm always around. I provide security and guide people around. My job is to protect and I'm always around for help." He winked.

Parth was puzzled again. Whatever the strange security guard was saying didn't make much sense to him and was completely difficult to believe.

Parth pondered, "How could anyone say he was always around? Didn't that sound like arrogating too much to one's self?" The words coming from the guard just did not sound like the words of a regular security guard.

"What's your name?"

"I'm Prabhudas. I work here as a security guard."

"But I've never seen you around here."

"Well you might have overlooked my presence. A lot of people do, but I'm always around."

"This way son." Prabhudas showed Parth a way towards the stairs that would lead them down to the last floor, from where they would take the Elevator.

When the elevator opened at the ground floor, Parth and Prabhudas walked out.

"Come, let's have a cup of coffee, tea or drinks. Would you like that?" Prabhudas asked.

"Sure, it's a great idea."

Parth was constantly feeling that something strange was happening. In the first place, he was not supposed to be alive. The commercial building had the least security, and Parth wasn't expecting any guard wouldn't be so occupied as to now be free enough to find him. This stranger also had a striking aura. Such strange things were known to take place only in movies, fantasy novels and mythical stories of legends. Parth was listening to him in fascination and it was almost as if only the words coming from this stranger could sooth his pain. It felt like cold water was cooling off the intense heat in his head which today had become a boiling cauldron of all the disappointment, resentment and depression that poured into his soul over these years.

Prabhudas also had an element of care and love to his voice that Parth could feel. His voice was strong and steady, and Parth felt as if he had known him for a long time. Besides, Prabhudas seemed wizened by insight, experience and his advanced years of adulthood. He had a strong physical build, looked fit and yet assumed a fatherly posture conveniently.

*   *   *

Prabhudas ordered for coffee while Parth took a lemon drink, he wanted the taste of lemon.

"Where do you stay?" Prabhudas asked Parth while sipping his coffee.

"I stay at Andheri, about thirty minutes from here."

Looking at Prabhudas, Parth had not thought of who would foot the bill. They were just taking drinks, but Parth was in a bad place. The worst was that he wasn't expecting any salary anymore. The financial strain had made Parth think a thousand times how he was going to manage things at home.

"I didn't want to live, but here I am with this old security guard and likely going to pay for his coffee bill to thank him for saving the same useless life I didn't want." Parth was cursing inside.

The waiter came with a bill and Prabhudas asked him straight away.

"Do you accept AMEX?"

"Yes Sir, we do" said the waiter who took the credit card given to him by Prabhudas.

"What the hell is AMEX and is this card stolen?" Parth was trying to glimpse at the name written on the credit card that Prabhudas gave the waiter to settle the bill.

The name on the card spelled "P R A B H U" and validity date looked something like 12/9999.

Parth was a bit taken aback to see something that looked that disturbing. Credit cards or debit cards to his knowledge usually had a valid through year only a few years away from current date and no one was ever issued such a small name as "P R A B H U"

"Prabhu had a literal meaning. The GOD."

Parth believed this was all a dream. Everything that had happened in the last forty-five minutes was totally beyond what Parth could explain or comprehend. Every little detail about Prabhudas was different and strange and hard to believe.

"Where do you stay?" Parth asked

"At the temple complex in the next lane."

But Parth had a lot of concerns of himself that he decided to ignore the strange observations, they were perhaps all just happening in his head. Prabhudas had saved his life and he was trying to make sense of his intriguing words. He just wanted to listen while he figured out what next to do with his life. He decided to just flow with the conversation while it lasted, while he contemplated facing his family.

After a few silent moments Prabhudas asked Parth.

"So what happened? What made you lose all faith?"

"My life was at a dead end. Nothing I do ever works. I only got by in college. My heart got broken. I got an average job after a long search. Now I have been fired. I have nothing in life to look forward to."

"Talking about your job, you loved it that much?"

"No I didn't even like it at all."

"Then why do you feel so severe for losing it?"

"Because I need to take a salary home every month to be able to support my family. I don't know how much the compensation I was promised will be."

"Do you think that job was the only way?"

"Well it looked like the only way, couldn't find any other."

"Always remember the end of one road is the beginning of another and often better one."

Parth felt a lot of positivity in that statement and kept listening to what Prabhudas had to say. He was hungry for words of hope and encouragement. He had hoped for Ashwini to do that for him, to give him the joy and hope he needed to pursue life some more. But now he had nothing and no one. He felt he could as well get as much words of strength as he could from Prabhudas.

"And talking about your broken heart...Did you love her?"

"Yes I did."

"Wow, sorry about that, must have really hurt. So how did you know you loved her?"

"It was the way I felt about her. I just couldn't get her out of my mind."

"Did she feel the same way about you?"

"No she did not."

"I thought so. You see for it to be love, it has to come full circle. It takes two to tango. You had feelings for her no doubt, but she didn't feel the same way about you. It was one sided and therefore incomplete. You couldn't have forced yourself on her."

"Then what was it? I felt it deep down in my soul, but she didn't reciprocate it."

"Well, it's the ego that you broke not your heart son. You felt bad that your strong feelings and many hours of adoration didn't matter to her. Your ego was badly bruised because you felt shamed and rejected."

"How can you say that?" Parth had a spark of anger in his eyes.

"Because all you really cared about Parth was how you felt and not about what she felt. You didn't consider her feelings before making your move. Now that she told you she didn't feel that way, you should have respected her feelings, but instead you sank."

"But then what could I have done to make her feel that way."

"Love does not work that way son. You should allow things happen naturally and at each person's pace. You should allow love grow. But if it never happens, you shouldn't force it. Look at the couple over there." Prabhudas pointed towards an old couple having quite a romantic tete-a-tete. It looked like they had been together for at least 30-40 years, yet they were so happy.

"Do you see that they are still having palpable romance after so many years? They are mutually happy and they are together."

Parth was silent. He was trying to think of what point Prabhudas was making.

"Now look the other way Parth, towards the waiter. Do you see that pretty girl over there?" Prabhudas was now pointing towards a girl sitting close to the waiter. She was very beautiful, had lovely eyes and long hair.

"She is fine."

"Well she has been eyeing you for a while now. I have caught her looking your way too often, something is up son. She fancies you."

"You know what? ...All of this looks too sudden, strange and too easy. I better begin to think of how to face my parents."

"Why not keep looking at her for some time. See if you like her too."

"What are you saying?"

"Don't be stubborn and don't feel so embarrassed boy. Ask yourself if you like what you see and if you feel attracted."

"So? What if I do?"

"Then be open. Be open to at least get to know her. Get to know each other. See if there is chemistry."

"I can't afford another heartbreak old man. I have had enough for one day. I almost died remember?"

"Sshhh...I am not that old, just in my mid-40s. She won't mind. Just keep noticing her too for some time."

Parth was now feeling embarrassed. He was totally clueless about what Prabhudas was trying to prove. He had taken quick glances at her and "gosh! She looks so stunning" he thought.

He didn't want her to catch him looking her way. He was admiring her hair when she caught him. He felt like running away. Unfortunately she saw his shyness, he had nowhere to run. She stared back beaming with a friendly mischief in her smile.

"Now tell me if you have the same feeling about this girl as you had for the girl who you claim broke your heart."

"What??. No way."

"Wait a second. What if she comes to talk to you? She knows you are shy boy."

"Why would she do that??" Parth said in a whisper, straining forward towards Prabhudas, as though trying to talk some sense into him.

"Well, see now." Prabhudas smiled.

Parth was amazed to see this stunning beauty hadn't stopped smiling at him. And now she had gotten out of her chair and was coming directly towards him. Parth felt something inside his heart lurch. He wasn't sure what to do. He felt shy, shaky, felt good and confused—all at the same time. Every second he had spent with Prabhudas was becoming something else, was it all a dream? Could he rely on such a fast lane of activities to build a life?

"Hi. Can I borrow your pen for a while?" The beautiful girl said with a smile that gave Parth the feeling that he was almost falling in love for the second time.

"Yes sure." Parth offered her the pen and she went to sit back at her table, scribbling away on some pieces of documents.

"Do you feel like falling in love again?" Prabhudas asked.

"YES I DO!" exclaimed Parth as he answered Prabhudas with tears forming in his eyes.

He was slowly beginning to understand the point that Prabhudas was making. He practically felt the same rush of feelings he had felt for Ashwini, and it didn't really feel like Ashwini mattered that much anymore.

"What really is love?" He asked himself. Maybe he had been too fixated on ashwini without finding out if she felt the same way.

"You see Parth, you are young and developing. Your hormones are also developing into that of full maturity as a male. These feelings are sometimes a little bit the effects from the biological system, and the fact that it was your first time."

"What?" That went like a bouncer over Parth's head. But now he understood that the feeling that had made him go crazy over Ashwini was actually an attraction he had felt. An attraction he should have ascertained was mutual. That she didn't feel that way about him didn't mean he would not find love, because right here where he sat he was already feeling something for a complete stranger.

He thought to himself, "Maybe it's because her gestures are encouraging....but she definitely isn't a pushover...she looks like a serious woman who has just gotten a promotion or won a major deal."

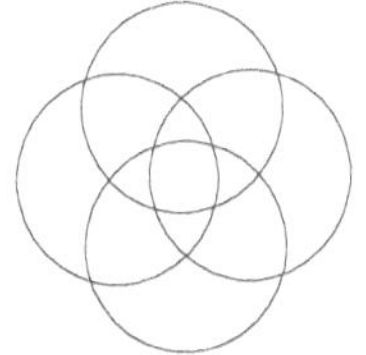

Chapter Three

Parth had now started smiling and his heart felt very light. He saw how crazy he was to have lost hope and faith in things that mattered in life, having known so little. Perhaps he was wrong about other things too. It was like all that had mattered to him, and for which he had wanted to take his life were only worth a huge laugh right now. Tears formed in his eyes yet again.

"Make sure to get back your pen son, and make sure to get much more than that. Let's meet again tomorrow say for 9am. My shift is later in the day, was only here for some paper work and to stand in for someone."

"But I don't know what to tell my family yet. How do I confront them with all of this?"

"Tell them when you are ready. You don't have to be in a hurry".

Parth started staring at Prabhudas again, asking how he could feel very comfortable with a complete stranger—one who had brought him back to life.

"How will I find true love and be successful in life? How will I be able to provide a good life for my family?"

"Son…love is something that you feel from the bottom of your heart. And when you find it, you won't be alone in the loop. It is not the loud superficial rush of emotions and hormones, but a deeper connection of friendship and a mutual decision between two people. Your problem is nothing but the lack of patience. With time you will understand it."

Parth suddenly felt there was someone else in the conversation; he looked to his side to see the beautiful girl standing by and smiling at him.

"How much of this had she heard?" he asked himself.

"Sorry, I didn't want to interrupt…I felt like you were both discussing something really important."

Prabhudas exchanged pleasantries with their new friend and told her his name.

"Do you mind making new friends?" he had asked her, "Looks like we need some new friends in our circle, especially those with such stunning beauty as yours", he remarked, putting Parth on the spot.

"Of course not. I love meeting new people. How are you? Do you work around here?"

"Yes I do. I am a guard at the "New Gate" Tower."

"Oh really, that's nice."

"Well you now know a bit about me, so what's your name?"

"I am Krisha."

"Krisha it's nice to meet you, this is Parth; Parth meet Krisha. Why don't you two get to know each other? Would have loved to hang out with you guys, but I have some paper work I need to sort out at the office right away. If you aren't busy this weekend I would ask what you think of all of us getting to hang out Saturday evening at the movies and then we grab a bite afterwards at my favourite spot?"

"Well I guess I am free this weekend, if that's ok with Parth?"

"Trust me Parth is in."

"Why speak for me, I am right here old...sorry... man."

"Yeah I can see that, just like I see the giggle on your face. "

"Krisha, let me do you the honours, please take your seat". Parth holds out the seat he had been sitting on and got her comfortably seated.

"Do you mind seeing me off to the door Parth?"

"Excuse me Krisha please give me a minute"

"That's fine Parth, don't take too long."

"You bet I won't keep him long." Prabhudas said with a witty smile.

"Parth, you have to be patient enough to find the things you truly love and everything will be fine. When you find your love and passion, your personal and career life will both take shape. Life will have a new meaning for you. Just take it one step at a time."

"How will love give me success?"

"Let's talk about that tomorrow, I would see you at 9am. Is that fine?"

"Yeah, I guess so."

*   *   *

As Parth walked back to his seat, he asked himself what he was supposed to do with all that was unfolding. Did he stand a chance with Krisha? Should he hope for so much? He remembered the words of Prabhudas and told himself he was just going to take it one step at a time. He wouldn't let the adrenalin rush and attraction get the better of him again. Let him get to know her first, and then they could see how things would progress.

"Hi Krisha, sorry to have kept you waiting."

"Not a problem Parth, that was quite fast. You two seem quite close."

"Yeah, we are I guess."

"What do you mean you guess? Is he your dad?"

"Ehm…nothing really. Sorry, never mind, we are actually close, but he is not my dad."

"Well I know we just met actually, I shouldn't get that nosy."

"Come on it's not a problem Krish, its fine. You seemed busy the other time; hope you aren't late for an appointment or something?"

"Nope, not at all, actually I just got a break-through after over two years of a tough pursuit. I have just secured funding for a major project from some important investors. I was signing some of the documents I am handing in tomorrow, wanted to read through every page before appending my signature. I also felt I should do it in a neutral place and not at the office."

"Wow congrats, that's huge. I am happy for you."

"Really? You are happy for me? You are just saying that, you barely know me. Anyway thanks for being nice."

"I guess we can truly be happy for people, if we ourselves know what it means to catch a big break. Trust me I have been down that route when it looks like nothing good will ever come or that your dreams are farfetched—and then suddenly things change."

In his mind Parth was literally shouting "I know that feeling! Because that's what I strangely feel now! …it feels like I just got back from the dead and I feel good…so I know what it is like to be happy for someone who just caught a break."

Krisha was wondering what Parth must have been through. Though she had really pursued this breakthrough, and at a point she was thinking she might never make it. She had refused to call in favours from her father, she wanted to earn her own way and not live in his shadows. This was especially after she discovered two of the men she had fallen in love with had turned out to be in love with her family's fame and status. She had been naïve. But it had now been over two years since she left that life behind and it had been tough.

She had dropped the family name, just so she could earn her way by merit. When she saw Parth walk into the restaurant with the guard, she was surprised at the perplexed look on his face. His hair was a bit rough, his shirt partly out at the side and his tie hung loosely from his neck. He didn't seem to care who was looking, yet his steps seemed cautious. She could tell he was in some form of trouble, but he also seemed locked in rapt attention with what this security guard was saying. Was that his father? It would be nice to see father and son relate so closely in such a real way.

Where she had come from, everyone had to put on their best behaviour. You couldn't be caught off-guard even if the worst thing was happening in your life. You always had to have it together and stick to what you wanted. It was why she had thought those relationships were real. She really felt it was what they had wanted. But she was wrong, they wanted something different, and her father had known all along. He had opposed her first man, but now she knew he had wanted something in return from the second relationship, that was why he had been open to it.

The worst part was her father thought she understood all that was happening, and why he had opposed the first relationship—exposing Aahan's other affairs. Aahan had tried to convince her they were all in the past, but she couldn't believe that it was love for her that had made him leave a year old relationship just a week after she showed up on the joint project. Like his name, he had this glory and freedom about him, she had been carried away.

She loved the corporate politics and corporate life, but she wanted passion that was real, a separation of corporate politics from family life. She felt swindled in her second relationship when she overheard her father and Aanav her second lover talking business over their marriage as a covenanted leverage for a lifelong partnership. They had truly fallen in love, but she just couldn't go through with it after that.

Khan had been making good efforts at the office lately, she could swear that she saw sincerity in his eyes and there was chemistry between them, but she wanted to be sure of who he really was outside of the corporate life. She knew he could tell she was someone important, though he couldn't lay his finger on the fine details. But the fact she knew his family and she didn't seem impressed by it got his attention. However, she had seen how he manipulated his way to getting the last committee appointment and she wondered if he was really different from the rest. She loved his drive and leadership abilities, and he seemed quite different, but was she willing to take the risk? She wasn't going to allow her emotions lead this time. But here was Parth, down-to-earth, real, showing his confusion...

"Are you okay? You seem lost in thought" Parth asked.

"Sorry, I was just reminiscing on things" she said.

"Did you close early from work today? Or are you also on a shift?"

"No…Yes, I did…I closed early at work" he lied.

"Oh I see. I guess you work in the same complex with Prabhudas?"

"No I don't", he said truthfully. "I only came to say hi. I had a lot on my mind so I came to bear it all out", he lied again.

"So what do you do?"

"Well, I do stuff. I am in sales…ehm actually…I interact with customers to see if they like to take our offers…"

Krisha could tell he wasn't comfortable giving out those details; she didn't want to press further.

"I work as an independent consultant with a Multinational firm in the image and corporate social responsibility arm of the company, while I am also an art collector and dealer. I am trying to make a difference through my work." She hoped he didn't feel intimidated by what she had said.

"You really sound intelligent and confident. Your ambition also seems well toned with a social face to it."

Parth wondered if Krisha was different from Ashwini, they both seemed ambitious and sociable, there didn't seem to be much of a difference except that he could really feel that Krisha was a part of this discussion for real. It wasn't just a friendly gesture, it was a lively and real one. She was really present and really talking.

"I ordinarily shouldn't say this, but you are really a beautiful woman and I really would love us to be friends. I mean real friends. I was wondering if I could call you sometime before Saturday just to say 'hi'?"

Why did he have to say "Real friends"? Hope he wasn't being too forward and putting her under undue pressure? "Parth, when will you ever learn?

"Sure Parth, I only like real things and real people, so I would love that. I guess that's an ingenious way of asking for my number, right?" They both smiled.

"And I like it when you call me Krish, you are really a good communicator."

She smiled knowingly as she said that and scribbled her personal line on a piece of sticky note which she gave to him.

Parth asked where she had parked, but she said she had taken a cab to work that morning. She needed to think clearly on the way to work.

He walked her to where she could get a cab, and said his "see you on Saturday" as the cab drove her off.

*   *   *

As Parth walked down the street of his house, it was already dark. His mum had called severally while he was on the bus, but he couldn't pick, he wasn't ready. There was a bit of traffic, but it cleared quickly. He sent her a text that he was on his way home and was tired from a long and hectic day.

He usually came home earlier, and he knew they would ask questions. He didn't want to arouse their suspicion. He looked so tired. That was enough to get them to leave him in peace, so he could rest. He had an appointment with Prabhudas for Nine 'O Clock the following morning, so he could as well get ready as though going to work. He wasn't ready to tell his parents what had happened. He at least wanted to get back his composure first, and know what he was doing. His former boss had paid for lunch, so he used what he had saved from his lunch money to buy some something for them to snack on. He just wanted to take a shower and retire for the night.

Parth knew his mum, her instincts will pick up something suspicious and her first thought would be the job. He was sure the only person she could call was his friend Subhash, so he knew he had to prepare Subhash ahead. He sent him a text.

"Hi Subhash, how are you today? Thanks for the heads up on the job and for all you do. I got fired at work today. I didn't have a good handle on things, but I am really doing great. Trust me I am fine and I am really on to something great. My mum will likely call you. Don't lie, but please don't disclose this just yet. Just tell her the last time we spoke I was very fine and there were no problems. That's all I ask. I want to tell them when I am ready. Trust me I got this. I will keep you posted".

Parth tried to sound jovial and hopeful in order not to also get Subhash worried. He pressed the send button and deleted the text. He didn't want to leave a trace. His mum always spied on him, he wanted to leave her no clues.

He thought of saying thank you to Prabhudas, but as he tried to type, he realized he hadn't collected his number.

"How could I miss that?" he thought, "Krish must have had something on me there for me to have forgotten to take his number."

As he thought of Krisha he typed "It was really a great experience with you today Krish. I was blown away. I look forward to another exciting moment with you. I just got home. Let me know if you are home yet. Have a great night."

Few seconds later as he was about to open the door, his phone beeped.

"Thanks Parth, I am home. I also had an amazing time hanging out with you handsome. And it was cool meeting Prabhudas, he is an interesting person it seems. I look forward to our Saturday hangout. Night night."

He wasn't going to delete their conversation. He now had something with which to distract his mum and family.

"Oh my son! You are back. Welcome home darling, how was work today? You are quite a bit late today and you look so tired. Is everything alright?"

"Of course I am fine mum. Just tired, had a long day. I got this for you all."

"Come on sweet Subhada, let the young man be, don't you see he is tired?", Abhay said.

"Hi dad, hey Tj, are you guys good?"

"ha ha, I am bubbling son, good to see you."

"I am fine bro." Tejas, Parth's younger brother replied.

Parth pulled off and went to the bathroom to take his bath. When he got back, his mum had set dinner before him. He ate, sat with the family for a few minutes and retired for the night.

*   *   *

Parth heard the door close stealthily. He looked at the time, it was 3am. He knew who just left the room. It wasn't a thief, it was his mother. As always, her curiosity had gotten the better of her and she had come to spy on him. She wanted to unravel what it was that made him look so distracted and withdrawn. She saw through the situation and believed Parth was avoiding conversations or had a couple of things on his mind he wasn't ready to talk about. She knew he didn't want to be caught unawares.

Parth decided he would lead her on. All she could get was the text he had sent to Krisha and her reply. Parth began to question whether all that had happened the previous day was a coincidence. It looked like those stories of mystical visitations that he had heard many times. As he began to ruminate on the events of the last twenty-four hours, a lot of questions flooded his mind.

"Is there really a divine order to this universe? Are there established rules that govern life? Hmmnn..."

"Parth, maybe there is a divine interest in your case after all. You have prayed for many years, but you weren't really clear about life...So what were you really praying about all those years if you knew so little? …You should have been praying more for guidance and courage."

Things felt different for Parth, especially now that he had just returned from the dead. He wondered what meaning his life would have had if he had died. What purpose it would have served? His family would have mourned sorely. Perhaps they would have discovered he was sacked, and would have felt they put too much pressure on him. That may have made them advocates against family-induced pressures. "But what pressure did they really put on me? They have been there for me, for us" he said to himself.

He had never really spoken about his desires. He had been too frigid. No doubt, the family looked up to him to help make its burdens bearable, but that was as far as they went. He too had always felt the need to be there for his family—it was the human thing to do. But nobody ever said he couldn't choose his own path on that journey. He had always been allowed to make his decisions.

Whatever pressure he may have felt from his parents to take on a particular career, was perhaps just their own way of providing guidance on what they thought was the best way possible. They never really could have thought they were sacrificing his happiness, because he had never really shown them any other way he might have preferred. Right from his tender years, his parents never forced anything on him.

Parth had to admit he had never really portrayed himself enough as an adult; he didn't yet seem decisive about anything. He instead had a hazy approach to life which diluted his focus and gave him a pessimistic disposition. This left-off an impression on those close to him that he was not enterprising, though no one could call him lazy—he somewhat didn't fit into the description of the lazy type. He just lacked that spark that could make him really pursue something or be energetic about his pursuits.

Parth looked again at the clock and it was 4:40 am. He yawned and turned to the other side of the bed, hoping to catch some more sleep so he could really be fresh when meeting Prabhudas. Parth was now beginning to believe that Prabhudas was a priest or special being sent at the right time for his help. As he thought about Prabhudas, he drifted to sleep.

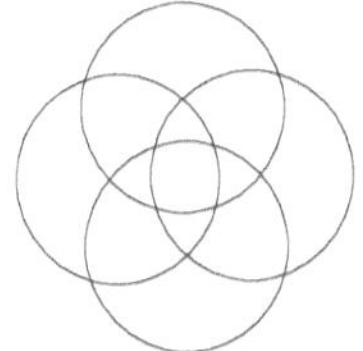

Chapter Four

"Something tells me you are for real" Krisha said.

"Krisha, you see it looks like I have learnt more in the last few hours than I have all my life. I am learning to be decisive and not to assume."

"I see…so am I assuming things?" She smiled.

"No Krish, I would rather say, I am the one prone to assumptions". Parth could feel his own fear.

What if he said something to show he had feelings for her and it again turned out to be pre-mature? Though they seemed attracted to each other, but he would rather wait things out this time.

"You have been badly hurt it seems. Who hurt you?"

"Let's just say, I hurt myself. I assumed there was something when there was none. I fantasized about it for so long that it became real to me. I was selfish."

"Wow, easy dude…don't be so hard on yourself Parth…she was your first crush I guess?"

"Is that what people mean by having a crush?"

"Well you could crush on someone but they may not feel the same way about you. It's better to be guided and not get hurt in such situations. You give it time, but if you can't see a clear-cut sign, you painfully have to let it go on time and not obsess about it. Obsessions take their toll and can be scary. You must know when the other person does or doesn't feel the same way."

"How do you identify a clear-cut sign that the person does?"

Krisha laughed and said, "Well I guess the way I am currently looking at you…and the way you are looking at me…the fact that we feel like holding each other's hands and saying sweet things to…ea…ch…"

"Parth! You are going to be late for work! Its 7:30am already!" Subhada shouted as she banged the door.

"Well you would be responsible if I am late; you disturbed my sleep mum! Besides, my appointment is for 9am…ehm…actually 8am".

He had mistakenly spoken about an appointment for 9am instead of his normal resumption time at work. He jumped out of the bed, and took out his clothes for the day from the closet. He proceeded to brush his teeth, thoroughly rinse his face and hair, after which he put on his clothes and started making to leave for his appointment.

"What do you mean I disturbed your sleep?"

"Mum you were in my room, how could you think I wouldn't know? Well I have always known for as far back as possible", he blurted.

Subhada looked shy as she walked toward him. He walked toward the verandah to spread his towel.

She had been caught. "You mean all these years you knew each time I had sneaked into your room?" She asked in surprise.

"Yes mama", Parth smiled mischievously as he walked back into the living room, "I hope you got what you wanted this time?"

"I love you son, I just wanted to know what was on your mind".

"I am fine mum. Trust me I know what I am doing", he smiled again, holding her shoulders, trying to reassure her. He strolled back to his room to pick something as he thought to himself if he actually knew what he was doing?

"So when are we going to see her sweetheart? Bring her home soon, I am eager to meet her", she said audibly enough to make sure he heard her. At this point Abhay echoed loudly from the other room that he looked forward to meeting her also.

"Well don't get excited you guys, there is nothing for now. We are just friends", Parth echoed back so his dad could hear.

Parth called out to his brother, who by now laid on the bed half-asleep and half-awake.

"See you later bro, I promise we would have our time".

They shared the same bedroom, but he was a deep sleeper, though he often slept late.

"Alright guys see you later", he said to his dad and mum as he approached the main door.

It was 7:50am when Parth left home. He was now reminiscing on the dream his mother had just interrupted with her loud call. Krisha had looked so breathtaking. Even now he still felt the awe of her aura. He wished he hadn't woken from the dream, and wondered how his brother could still sleep after such a disturbance.

Krisha had said quite a lot in his dream. What was he to do with all of that? He wondered. Well he would just take it one step at a time, though it did seem like the attraction was mutual. He remembered how she kept stealing looks at him before she asked for his pen the previous day at the café.

Now, as he looked back, he wondered how she could have left home for such an important day without a pen. He smiled—she must have had a pen in that fancy purse of hers. He felt he should compose a text to wish her the very best for the day.

"Hi Krish. Hope you had a great night? After listening to you yesterday, I have no doubt whatsoever that you are indeed a great and exceptional woman. You also have this immaculate beauty and charming smile. Our world is lucky to have you. Have an awesome day Krish. Talk to you later".

He pressed the send key.

*   *   *

Parth arrived at 8:40am.

He was happy he had some twenty minutes before Prabhudas showed up. This gave him some time to brood on the questions he wanted to ask, while recollecting discussions from the previous day. He asked himself again what he really wanted from life.

"How do you know that you are on the right track or that you know what you are doing? There has to be a way to know, or parameters to judge by."

These were the things bothering his mind and it seemed like it applied to a variety of areas in his life. How could he tell that Krisha would be the right person for him?

Parth was occupied with his thoughts when Prabhudas walked into the café. Parth noticed the solidity of his build, the certainty in his steps, and the liveliness in his face. They smiled at each other, exchanged pleasantries and had their seats. Parth could see the sparkle in Prabhudas' eyes. The clarity and radiance in his eyes had such a vitality that put one at ease and gave Parth the impression that he was in the presence of a wise one.

"So tell me about Krisha"

"Oh…yeah Krisha. She is stunning, serious about life, and…ehm"

"…attracted to you" Prabhudas cut in. "Though she seems absorbed and energetic about what she does don't you think?"

"Yeah, but how do you know that? You were barely here for how many minutes?"

"Well I saw enough to decode that. The way she looked at those documents and kept smiling, it looked like she had just got a breakthrough after some tedious work. And she couldn't take her eyes of you either…"

"You keep saying that, but I had better take your advice…one step at a time."

"Just make sure it is the right step, don't miss your moment."

"I even had a dream about her…I really have to be careful. I am already falling for her…but what if all she wants is friendship? I can't afford to go down that hole of mistaken love again and get myself drowned".

"Listen son, love doesn't have to be complicated. When two people find true love, it is like a new bust of liquid energy that begins to grow in their hearts and that they feel in their body. As they both begin to recognize the pull towards each other, it also comes alive with a new meaning, unending bubbles of joy and a new mutual succour. Beyond the rush of emotions, they feel a new meaning to life, and they see a future they don't want to miss."

"All of this sounds too philosophical for me."

"It's quite simple Parth, it is as though a lost part of their lives has been found. They are electrified by the collision of their mutual energy and fondness. This in turn creates a whole new world of happiness, meaning and peace for them. This is why it must be mutual. For some, all of these things come together and are tested in only a matter of hours and days, while for many it could take weeks, months and even a year or more, to arrive at that point of conviction where they are ready to plunge in. Bottom line is, both of them must be convinced and enraptured."

"Wheeew…that's really interesting and enlightening. Yesterday, you said something about love and success; I can't seem to relate to how love brings success. How does that work?"

"Again Parth, it's simple. You have to find a job that you love. You must find something that you feel really happy doing. You know…you like the moment of it…you can do it with an excitement every day… and jump right out of your bed every single morning or at night just because of it."

"That sounds great. I've always wanted to do that. But how do I find that out?"

"We would talk about that, but we have barely touched our food. Let's eat so we can enjoy the rest of our conversation."

Parth couldn't stop asking Prabhudas these questions, Prabhudas exuded a confidence and certainty that captivated him, and every answer Prabhudas gave sounded like a perfect explanation to the question. It really made a lot of sense to him. He wished he had known these things earlier, he would perhaps have made better choices in college and would never have faced the embarrassment with Ashwini. He couldn't believe all of this had almost cost him his life. He had been naïve and undiscerning.

They finished their cups of *Jal Jeera* and ate their *Bedmi Puri* served with *Raseele Aloo.* It proved quite a tasty serving, and they soon found themselves talking about their favourite cuisines and culinary skills. Parth talked about how poor he was at cooking and how he had managed to only learn a few dishes well. Prabhudas seemed to be saying he could do some really good cooking and looked forward to inviting Parth over if they had the opportunity.

Parth was also curious about Prabhudas' family. Did he have a wife? Did he have children?

"Well Parth it's really a long story. I will tell you some of it now, but the rest you will find out later"

"I have been in love for many years now and it has been an amazing journey. I still cherish the very beginning of my love journey because of the indescribable joy the idea brought to my heart at the time—a joy I still feel even now. Apart from having a rewarding journey with my perfect partner, the other part of it that has thrilled me has been the unique opportunity to set in motion the birth of human lives through child bearing. I love my children and I have quite a large family. We started early, and I and my beloved are dedicating time to nurturing our children, to spend time with them and ensure they are guided in their life choices, especially for the younger ones who trust our wisdom. It's part of why I am in Mumbai."

Parth was thrilled by the narrative. Prabhudas truly seemed like a wise and caring father. What Parth was a bit curious about was why Prabhudas didn't seem eager to talk about his wife, and why he used formal terms like partner and beloved. But one thing he got clearly was that he and this beloved of his had given birth to quite a number of children. Parth felt he had known enough for one day, he didn't want to push it any further.

They listened to the midday news at the café. Prabhudas wanted to engage Parth some more.

"Let's take a walk son."

"Sure." Parth was excited to continue with the hang out.

By this time, it was well past midday. The sun was up and the sky was bright. The area was well shaded by the tall office buildings and trees. The walk was peaceful. Parth was enjoying the company of Prabhudas. The conversation a few minutes ago started coming back to his mind.

"When you find what you love, your personal and career life both will be fine."

As Parth chewed on these thoughts, the curiosity and questions gradually started flowing again.

"You said doing what I love is the key to success. I get that. But what I still don't get is how I can find what I love."

"Let me get back to that", Prabhudas said.

Parth and Prabhudas at this time were walking past a brand new four-star hotel that had just opened in the area two months earlier. Parth had heard about the hotel and had zoomed past a couple of times it in a bus or taxi, but standing right in front its elegance caught his attention in a new and unique way. Prabhudas noticed Parth's distraction and asked if he had ever been this close to the hotel. Parth told him he hadn't. They caught just a glimpse of the lobby, but in that one glimpse it all looked so homely and mesmerizing.

"It looks like there is some event going on here." Parth noted from the number of people and cars in the hotel premises. He always had a curiosity about successful people, their lifestyle and especially their cars.

The grand entrance of the hotel was well decorated and had an allure in its lighting.

"Look Prabhudas, it's the new BMW X6! What an amazing car!" Parth was pointing towards a car that was just coming out of the hotel's entrance.

"Oh God! Can you see him? I can't believe it. Look it is Sachin Tendulkar. Wow, look at him. I've always watched him on TV but I have never seen him from such a close distance."

As the car was slowly getting out of the compound, the windows were still open and the face of Sachin Tendulkar sitting inside the car could easily be seen.

"Tendulkar is one of the world's finest cricketers and a very successful man."

"So what do you know about Sachin Tendulkar?"

"Oh, he plays great cricket and he is very successful and rich. Did you look at the BMW X6? That car costs Rs. 85 lacs."

"So why do you think he is successful?"

"He is so rich. He has a big house, rides an expensive car, he owns property and lives a very comfortable life."

"Son, what you are telling me are the signs of success. I'm asking you why you think he is successful in the first place."

"Because he plays great cricket."

"Why does he play great cricket?"

"Because he was born for cricket."

"Okay…you know what? Come with me, I want to show you a place not far from here."

"Where are you taking me?"

"It's not far from here, come on let's go."

Parth was curious about what was coming next.

"This bus will take us there." Prabhudas said pointing towards the bus.

Parth followed Prabhudas towards the bus. He asked for two tickets to oval ground, and got both of them seated.

*   *   *

It was about 1pm when they arrived and the heat was beginning to scorch. Unlike the business district where roads were shadowed by tall buildings and trees, this place was very open. Parth and Prabhudas had just gotten out of the bus and were walking towards a large sports ground where many teenage boys and girls were practicing various sports. They walked across the field, but the heat was much.

"Mehn it's getting quite hot out here. I can barely stand the heat. It is hot. I'm sweating. I need water." Their sudden entry into the field under the direct heat of the sun had caused Parth some sudden feeling of de-hydration and discomfort. He hadn't been under the sun this long in a long time. Even when he jogged, it was always early in the morning. He observed that Prabhudas looked relatively comfortable and was busy looking at the sportsmen and women with a fascinating smile.

"Here, take this. I have some." Prabhudas offered Parth the bottle of water he had bought when they were leaving the café."

"What about you? You knew we were coming here all along right?"

"I am fine son…well you could say that."

Parth broke the seal on the cap and took about three gulps.

"What do you think about the weather?"

"Oh it is hot and unfriendly."

Parth had pointed them to take shade under a refreshment stand close by.

"What do you think about those kids playing in the field under this weather?"

"I never thought of it. It's crazy kids stuff."

"Why would you say that? You don't play sports?

"I do sometimes, but that's in the evening, not in a scorching heat like this."

"So why do you think these kids are in the sun playing hard?"

"Because they want to be great sportsmen and women?"

"Well that's not all son. Don't you think those kids out there are loving it?"

Parth gave the expanse of field another look. He could see the kids loved the competitiveness of the game and most of them were playing with smiles, enthusiasm and energy. Parth also noticed how the kids were totally focused and had no feeling of worries. They were just happy being there at that moment.

A new consciousness was unfolding in Parth's mind. He moved a little bit out of the shadow and felt how difficult and uncomfortable it was to stand in the scorching heat that almost made him fall from dehydration. He was now beginning to learn the point Prabhudas was making.

"How can you say they are loving it?"

"Why else would they have themselves out there in this torturing weather and yet be smiling, happy and so focused on the game?"

"So you're saying when you love something, you will take any pain to do it?"

"Well, when you are in love, you don't really feel the pain of anything. You just love being there. You have no worries and you rarely think about anything else. Everything else just works out. Mind you it's just about 1pm, it will still get a bit hotter here."

Parth was feeling a strange peace inside his heart as Prabhudas continued his point.

"Now remember the famous and successful cricketer Sachin Tendulkar that you saw short while back. He was once a kid like these ones here spending their extra-curricular time doing what they love. When he was a kid, he too used to play in this weather almost every day. No matter what he just kept playing. Now think of it, that's what he does even today."

"And now he's successful."

"Love for sure is the foundation of success. But it's not the success itself. There are some more elements before one can become successful."

"Some more elements?"

"Yes. But let's try to find out about other successful people as well. Who else do you know that is successful?"

"Hmm...Amitabh Bachhan. He is a great actor and a very successful person."

"What do you know about him?"

"He has very big houses, big cars. People love him."

"Why do people love him?"

"Because he is a great actor."

"Why do you think he acts?"

"Because he loves to?"

"Exactly. That's the point I want to make. Will you like to visit the theatre to see a drama?"

"Now?"

"Yes, the drama theatre is just a few minutes' walk from here. We would find students and young performers there."

As Parth and Prabhudas walked towards the drama theatre, Parth could see various posters of drama that were scheduled to be acted at the theatre.

While Parth was looking closely at some of the posters, Prabhudas rushed to a ticket window.

"One starts in five minutes from now. Let's move in."

Parth was excited to see a drama. Although he had seen many movies on TV screens and in cinemas, He had never seen a live performance yet."

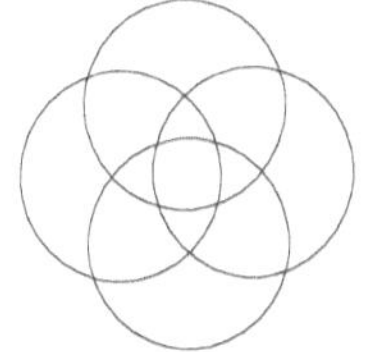

Chapter Five

"So, what do you think about the drama?"

"It was great. How could the actors focus on what they were saying in front of so such an audience? I didn't expect to see so many people too. How could the performers show emotions so realistically that were not their actual emotions?"

"The answer is same my son. It's the love they have for what they do. They love being actors. They love to act. They love to be in the moment of it without having feelings of worries or tensions. And that is why they can totally immerse themselves into expressing actions and reactions as required by the characters they take on."

Parth was nodding his head now. His mind was trying to grasp the depth of the feeling of love these performers had for their work. A feeling where one forgot all his tensions and worries and just focused on the moment and did the job every second, every day, every year and every time.

"Do you understand now why Amitabh Bachhan acts?"

"Yes, because he loves to and that's why he is so successful."

"Well he loves to act but success needs a few more elements which as I said I'll talk to you about—maybe at a later time. I want this first point to sink in."

"Similarly, I am sure you can you remember some other successful people?"

"Yes. Asha Bhosale loves singing, Michael Jordan loves Basketball. Nadal Federar loves tennis. Nigella Woods loves cooking. Businessmen and inventors are also very successful. They are rich, have big houses, ride big cars."

"Yes. Love goes the same way for them also. They love to create products that they can sell."

"Mention any famous inventor and businessman you know?"

"Steve Jobs."

"He loved creating the computers, mobile and music devices that he is known for."

"Yea, now I get the point. One cannot be successful in something unless he loves to do it."

"Correct. You're a fast learner son."

Parth's mind was now totally engaged. He could remember many successful personalities that were now flashing through his mind, and he saw now how they must have loved doing what they did.

But then suddenly Parth remembered the pain that he had gone through the previous day. At the back of one corner of his mind, he was having the good feeling of how he had learned just now about how successful and famous people loved what they do. In another corner of his mind, he was feeling the void of not being able to identify anything that he loved.

Parth began to question himself.

"I actually never took time to ask myself or to discover what I really love to do. The only thing I got up to think about every morning was how I was going to feed my family and solve the problem of money. Am I not unlucky to have been so caught-up under such pressures? So much so that I could not think for myself what I actually wanted to do with my life?"

Parth couldn't resist raising his concern.

"Don't you think it's difficult to find what you love sometimes when you have so much to look after?"

"True in one sense and false in another."

"What does that mean?"

"It means, it's difficult to find your love if you go along with the expectation of others and the noise around you. But, it's easy to find it if you are looking inwards to find it out regardless of the noise, just as I believe you are now doing." Prabhudas said with a wink.

Parth was suddenly embarrassed to face Prabhudas as he remembered how he had decided to quit life and give up. But on a second thought he made eye contact with Prabhudas and told him pointedly.

"I really want to find out."

This was a pain of over two years that Parth could no longer endure, and he was sure that he was not going to let any other factors control him again. He was going to find out what his destiny was, what his love was.

"The afternoon is quite spent now, my shift is later this evening. I had better start heading back to my place and freshen up for the night", Prabhudas said looking at his watch. It was past 4PM now and ever since Parth met Prabhudas from the day of the incident, he had hardly noticed how time seemed to fly so quickly in Prabhudas' company.

"Tomorrow is Saturday, and we are hanging out with Krisha, I believe it would be fun. Spend the morning with your family, and let's meet by 12pm at the Café as agreed. Make sure to be in touch with her ahead as a reminder."

"Yes I will", Parth answered with an excitement in his voice. He walked Prabhudas to the bus stop as they both waited briefly to each join a bus going to their different parts of town. "Bye, see you tomorrow", Parth said as Prabhudas waved back at him as their buses moved.

"buzz…buzz…buzz…buzz", Parth's phone was ringing, he had put his phone in vibration mode earlier. The caller ID showed it was Krisha, he was surprised because he was just going to call her.

"Hi dear, how are you?"

"I am fine Krish, how are you too?"

"I am good Parth, and thanks for the text this morning, it really was a good morale boost."

"Wow, I am happy to hear that Krish, it's a pleasure."

"So I was wondering if I could ask you for a favour?"

"Feel free Krish, would be glad to help."

"The paper work went well today and the further discussions were also a success. But I have no one to celebrate with. I was wondering if you wouldn't mind a drink or something. Do you mind?"

"That would be nice Krish, where can I meet you?"

"Let's meet at the café say in thirty minutes, and then we can go to my favourite spot. I have a favourite spot too", she giggled.

"Okay, that works for me. See you then."

"Thank youuuuuuuuu. See you then Parth."

*   *   *

After the bus had moved and Parth had settled in, he had been contemplating on how to broach the call to Krisha. What was he going to say on the phone? Of course there was the hangout the following day to talk about, but he had begun to feel like he wasn't giving Krisha enough breathing space. He remembered how he sent Ashwini several messages without getting any replies. He didn't want to be seen again as that guy who disturbed unreasonably. He should look out for clues before leaping into the pool. He had been thinking for about ten minutes when his phone buzzed with Krisha on the other end of the call. He reckoned that she was returning the gestures, which meant that they could at least be friends, and that really made things more bearable for Parth.

He was there five minutes early and waited for Krisha who walked in just a few minutes after he got there. He couldn't believe his eyes. Krisha had dressed down a bit by taking off her coat and un-tucking her fitted long sleeve shirt. She looked smart and relaxed. The glint in her eyes was disarming.

She was out of this world, and he could feel the warmth sweetly rising in his belly that he was grinning from ear to ear when he got up to greet her.

"Wow! Congrats girl! So proud of you."

"Hi Parth, thanks for coming!" They hugged briefly while Krisha motioned to the taxi she had waiting outside for them.

"I got a taxi waiting for us outside."

"Alright, great."

During the drive, Krisha chatted about her day and how actually hectic it had been, though she had enjoyed every bit of it. They hadn't driven for long when they arrived at the four-star hotel Parth and Prabhudas had seen earlier.

"Oh really is this the place?"

"Yeah, you know this place?"

"Not really, had heard of it but never had a close look until earlier today when I and Prabhudas walked by."

"Oh your guardian angel brought you hear?"

"Well we just walked by, the place looks beautiful, I wonder why it isn't a five-star hotel"

"Well I hear they are almost there. The rating might change before the year runs out. A lot of staff training, varieties of menus, room upgrades, suites modeling and other logistics are being put in place."

"You seem to know quite a lot, are you one of their consultants?"

"Not really, we used their facilities recently and I was impressed with the professionalism. But what caught my attention is that the manager is a lady. I just loved the fact that there was no gender bias in choosing who could run the place. And so I took more interest and even offered advice."

"I see; it's the solidarity thing right? That's cool."

"I believe in humanity Parth, and I believe god designed women to contribute their own part to humanity's growth and beauty. So when I see women allowed to express their gifts, I am usually impressed. I am not some extremist, but I believe in balance and the dignity of womanhood."

"Wow! You almost got me there. I just might join your campaign. In fact I am in. I share your thoughts too."

"Wow that's cool. It feels good to have the support of people you care about." Krisha had practically pouted after she said that.

"Well I figured that since you came to celebrate with me, I could at least consider you my friend. I haven't got any around. I can call you that right?" she added after a brief awkward moment of silence.

Parth could see the shyness and flicker of embarrassment in her eyes and he wanted her to feel comfortable.

"Come on Krish, I am delighted to be your friend. To say the least I am spell bound by your charisma, sense of purpose, and flawless beauty. Now tell me, who would ever want to trade away such a lifetime opportunity to be your friend? You really inspire me."

There was a startling amazement written all over her face as she listened to Parth, she looked like she couldn't believe her ears. Parth thought he saw tears forming in her eyes. She quickly grabbed him for a hug to quickly pull back the tears. "Your words are remarkable and heart-warming Parth, thanks a million" she said, as she clung to him in the embrace for about thirty seconds.

Parth didn't have a sister, but he had seen at close call how many women had been relegated simply because they were women. He was lucky to have had a father who didn't share such sentiments and who respected his mother so much. His dad had even wanted her to advance her studies, but she had said she felt too old for that and had gotten too involved in her trade to pull back. She loved what she did. She had worked so hard, and had supported his dad in providing for the home, until the doctors said she had to take things easy.

She led him to her favourite corner where they sat. She placed her order. Parth simply asked for whatever she was ordering, he couldn't find his way around the menu.

"You called Prabhudas my guardian angel, why?"

"Well after you told me he wasn't your father, I was surprised at the bond you both shared. He seems like a wise man to me, and I envy you. It is a privilege to have someone who could offer you good counsel."

They made a toast to Krisha's new project and to their friendship. They chatted about family, love and their dreams. Krisha wasn't keen on talking about career, she didn't want to make Parth awkward, he clearly didn't seem enthusiastic about his career life. They soon strolled down the street and took two separate cabs as they retired home for the night. It was 6:45pm and Parth figured he would be home in about thirty minutes. He was at the door when Krisha's text came in.

"I am home and dry. Thanks for tonight."

"I had a great time too Krish, it was fun hanging out with you. See you tomorrow at the café for

12noon, Prabhudas and I can't wait to be captivated by your charm once again. Just got home too."

"Alright, good night."

As Parth was going to bed that night, he recollected the events of the day and kept thinking "I wasn't supposed to be alive today, but here I am having the greatest experience of my life."

He was excited about catching up with the mysterious Prabhudas the next day, and have Krisha's appearance as the icing on the cake. He had only met them in less than last 48 hours, but he felt like he had known them for ages.

"Tj, do you still do your weekend jogs? Do you mind jogging with me tomorrow morning?" Parth had asked his brother Tejas.

"Sure. I have never stopped jogging. Sound mind in a sound body is one of my hard lines. It also helps me reflect and think."

*   *   *

The following morning, Parth was up early. He woke with the same feeling of excitement. It was a big contrast from the way he had felt for many years. Looking back to those years, Parth could hardly remember ever feeling this excited at anytime. He couldn't also tell at what point he began to lose his enthusiasm for life. It was not that he didn't have times when he was happy and related with family and friends, but even when he did, there was this drab covering that he couldn't shake-off. He couldn't keep the excitement for long.

His life had changed quickly. What almost ended as a day of suicide because of depression had turned out into an avenue for new hope. He couldn't believe the sharp contrast.

Parth and Tejas stepped out of the house and jogged through the streets and their favourite routes. They had a short break and took time to catch up. Rohan talked about school and how he had managed to find his feet. He had come home because they had a break and were to take time to come up with a proposal before they were posted for some form of internship.

Tejas had preferred to come home to put together his thoughts and have the solitude of the room in the day to conduct his research. He would also enjoy the rapport of the family in the evenings to relax. He visited the library when he needed to and spent some time every evening catching up with friends on social media.

Parth was happy that his brother had an independent mind and some clarity about what he wanted.

He didn't seem dogmatic about anything, but neither was he clueless. Parth also saw how much Tejas needed all the support he needed to stay focused at school. He was convinced he needed to find a new job. He was going to squeeze out the information he needed from Prabhudas somehow. He felt that sense of responsibility again, only that this time he wanted to do something within the context of what he loved. Who knew if one day his brother would need his advice? He needed to be ready.

When they got home, it was 8:30 am. Parth quickly got some of his clothes ready for washing. He couldn't afford laundry services, so he had to do his laundry himself. He took out only the essential clothes so that he didn't have to spend so much time washing. His excitement still got the better of him and he wasn't compromising. Parth had still not spoken to his parents about anything. No one at home knew he had been fired from his job. He knew he couldn't hide it for long and he didn't want to put Subhash in an awkward position.

Subhash had told him that his mother had called, but that he hadn't told her anything, though he avoided lying he wasn't sure if he wouldn't crack next time. Parth had been in such a good mood after he came home that no one even suspected a thing.

Fastloan.com had paid him some form of compensation, and he had planned to give most of it to the family—though it meant he would have so little left.

"This looks like a master plan. My family could have been in a disaster of some sort only two nights ago if I had not come back at all, or if I told them about the job loss. I currently have no means of earning an income, but I believe there is a way out." Parth kept assuring himself.

After meeting Prabhudas, life had really turned around for him. This was what he had really wished for when he prayed—he had wanted a turnaround.

*   *   *

"Hi guys, good to see you two", Krisha had said as she bumped into Parth and Prabhudas at the entrance to the café.

Parth and Prabhudas expressed their happiness to see her as they exchanged pleasantries.

"Have we all had breakfast?" Prabhudas asked,

Krisha and Parth both nodded in the affirmative.

So they headed out to the cinema and chatted along the way.

Some minutes later, they arrived the cinema hall and joined the next movie session. They liked the movie title.

The movie lasted an hour and a half. They had a good time.

When the movie was over, they chatted about the story line as they walked out of the cinema premises.

Prabhudas stopped a cab and gave descriptions. All three were in the cab and off to a resort on the Madh Marve road, a little away from the bustling city centre.

It was fun talking about movies they had seen on the long drive.

The resort was a mixture of nature's beauty, artistic creativity, luxury and class.

There were other visitors and this made it more fun. But there was also the exclusivity that made them fall in love with the place.

Prabhudas showed them round the many sights before they settled down to lunch.

The cuisines were exquisite and this time Parth had the luxury to choose his favourite dish like everyone else.

The food was good.

They loved the scenic view of the resort as you came towards the main building. They sat in the open bar area where table and chairs were set overlooking the beautiful landscape of the resort and seeing new people coming in for their tourist stay. Obviously many of the families were from the middle and upper class that lived in neighbouring towns, one could tell from the cars which they came in.

Whenever a new car drove to the stop, Parth couldn't resist the urge to take a look. He seemed more inclined to leaving his ears behind in their conversation, while his eyes roved towards the metallic beauty before him.

Parth thought he could engage Prabhudas a bit. "Prabhudas, from our last conversation, you were trying to show me how to find what I love. Do you mind talking about that?"

"Well, you have to set yourself to it and give yourself time. And more than looking outside, it's the self questioning that really helps. Your observation of yourself. Loving what you do is not all you need to succeed, but it is the first key to success."

"Wow. That's really something…" Krisha quietly said with an awakened interest.

"You see, the Japanese have found an innovative coinage for it, they call it '*Ikigai*'—i.e. the reason for one's existence."

"Hmmmnnnn…so how does one develop a career from this?"

"When you locate your passion, i.e. something you are really attracted to or passionate about, the next thing is to become good at it—that way it is becoming a profession. If you can trace that to people's real needs or something people really want, and then you make it your mission to satisfy those needs or desires, you could as well get them to pay for it. At this point is when it becomes an occupation or vocation, i.e. something people are willing to pay you for."

When Parth got back to the conversation, he realized his ears didn't catch everything, he became frantic. "Ehm…sorry…eh…I missed that. Please could you kindly come again? I got it to the point where you become good at your passion, which makes you a professional, but that part on *'trace people's needs… something'*…sorry I missed that part."

"That's not a problem Parth, relax don't get worked up. But before I go over that again, what is it that often diverts your attention? I have noticed that quite often."

"When?"

Krisha mischievously looked at him with a comical face and said "Well Parth, right while we were talking. Undeniably, this conversation seems so dear to your heart, but it appears there is also something, or maybe some things, which you just can't seem to ignore. I have noticed too. Is there a special girl around somewhere?"

"Where? Here? No, save for you…ehm…sorry… well I don't know. I mean there is no girl anywhere."

"Well it's almost as if you have been watching something", Prabhudas added.

"Oh that? You mean that I have been looking at "s.o.m.e.things" and not "someone"? Well yes, it has been the cars. Mehn! Some of these folks have eyes for good cars! People are making quite some bucks around here."

"So you like watching them?"

"Oh I just love to. The amazing brilliance that goes into those machines is fascinating."

"Really? You really do seem captivated"

"Yes. Kind of."

"So do you want to be a driver?" Prabhudas asked?

"Well I like to drive mine someday but no. Not a driver. I just like watching them, knowing about them, reading about them, talking about them. I love to discuss their features, talk about their prices etc."

"Well there is a new multi car show room opened in the main city. They say it's one of the biggest, if not the biggest, in the city. Do you want to check them out?"

"Yes, I know the place, it's massive!" Krisha added.

"Wow Prabhudas, are you putting me up to something here? Do you know I never thought of that? Thinking about it now, it would really be fun."

"Well guys, I have to head back to my crib to freshen up for the night, my shift is closing in."

"Well I would really love to accompany you to the showroom Parth if you don't mind. Besides I didn't know you loved cars. From the showroom, we could head back to my place, I have one in my garage you won't get over, I promise."

"Really? Alright, let's do it Krish., I guess we had better start heading to the main city."

Parth and Krish waved at Prabhudas as he boarded a separate cab, while they took another. For a while they headed together in the same direction as they re-entered the heart of the city.

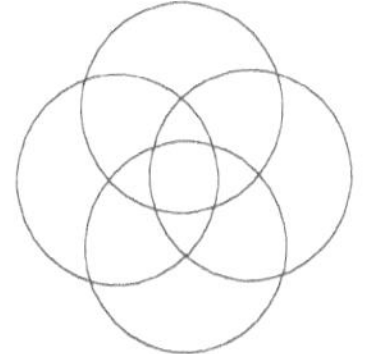

Chapter Six

Krish and Parth arrived at Pride Cars showroom.

"Wow, look at this, this is amazing. I have never seen a showroom as big as this."

Parth was awestruck as they got out of the cab as he looked towards the main building of the newly opened multi brand car showroom.

Pride cars showroom was a new concept in car dealership. It was massive. It was spread over an entire area like a campus. It had nearly 400,000 sq ft of space, part of which was used to test run vehicles or display their prowess. There was as much space available for visitors' cars as there was for the new cars themselves. Unlike the brand specific showrooms, this facility was showcasing cars from about eighteen car manufacturers. It was a one-stop-shop with facilities like loans, insurance and a car servicing center.

"Oh my god!! What an amazing place this is! How did you know about it?"

"Well they were in the papers when they opened, and besides our company was interested in getting some new vehicles."

"Really? How come I missed it then?"

"Well I don't know much. I am just getting to know you. Maybe Prabhudas would know right?" she winked and smiled.

"I am sorry this all feels awkward, I just wasn't ready to talk about how terrible my life has been, how I was naïve about love, and got fired from a job I practically hated but tried so hard to do and couldn't make headway. My life has been a mess."

"Hey, come on Parth, I think you are an amazing man. You are so real and that's so rare where I come from. Don't be so hard on yourself."

They entered through the main lobby and were checked in by the security guard. Parth was so over-whelmed by his ecstatic mood that he was carried away by the fleet and started checking them out.

"Oh..Look at that, that's the new Lexus. It's an automatic 250 bhp."

"And this one...the new...."

"And look at this..."

Parth was enamored as he kept talking about many of the cars as he walked through the aisles.

"This looks like a five star hotel for cars. And look at this car...the new..."

Parth went on nonstop.

Krisha was happy for him. He looked like he was going to burst. She could only imagine how much of that energy had been bottled up for years. She didn't want to spoil this moment, she wanted him to have his fill.

"You take a look, I'll sit in this chair here" Krisha told Parth, and grabbed an armchair to sit.

"Are you sure?"

"Of course Parth, I am so happy for you right now and I don't want you to miss this. I love your energy. I will also feed my eyes here, but I want you to let out this energy and I don't want to stand in the way one bit."

It was 5:25pm, and the showroom didn't close until 7pm, they still had time.

Time passed by as Parth immersed himself in the showroom. He was watching other customers looking at cars and asking questions about them. Parth closed in on many conversations of many of the customers to hear what they had to ask. The showroom was so big that you couldn't single out anyone in particular among the many customers.

Sometimes Parth helped out with the answer to a query by a customer when the customer service representative was unable to. And because the showroom was expansive and newly opened, it clearly had some shortage of customer care staff.

Parth was unaware of the time. He had also observed some of the policies and noticed that some customers were coming in to book their cars for staggered payment plans.

It suddenly struck Parth that Krisha was waiting for him, so he quickly tried to locate the place where he had left her. The showroom was so big that he had some difficulty locating the place at first. But Krisha noticed that he was looking for her and started to wave. When he saw her waving, he smiled and walked over to where she was.

"I am so sorry to have kept you waiting. I didn't notice the time. I am willing to walk you home."

"Come on Parth, its just 6:30pm, it's not that late. Though I would have loved you to stop by at my place, but I guess it's late. Do you want to come by tomorrow Sunday?"

"Yeah sure, that's fine."

Parth's phone rang, it was Prabhudas.

"Wow! The place is lovely old man."

"I told you I am not old young man. Is Krisha still with you? It's getting late."

"Yes, she is. I didn't realize that much time had passed. Though I offered to walk her home."

"Hey give me the phone, I am a big girl, I can take care of myself. Hi, wise man, how are you? You needed to see Parth, he seemed like he was going to burst from excitement."

"Oh really? It looks like he has found something he loves doesn't it?"

"I guess he has. Don't worry guys, I would be fine. I get home late most days. Trust me, my area is kind of safe."

"Alright, if you say so. You guys have fun, I am back at some work here."

"Bye"

"How about you come by my house at 4pm tomorrow? I would give you the address. I would rest a bit, do some laundry and prepare you a nice meal. What do you say?"

"Alright you win."

She wanted to get to know him better. Perhaps there was some chemistry between them that would be more obvious in an atmosphere of friendship, with just the two of them. But so far she couldn't help herself, she had fallen for him. His innocence, simplicity, large heart and athletic build were perfect for her. He seemed a bit withdrawn, but she could tell he looked at her specially. But her life wasn't stable yet it seemed.

Parth saw her off to a cab and waved at her as they said their good-byes for the night.

*   *   *

Parth felt a bit tired. It had been another great day with loads of new wonderful memories he was building, though the activities were also engaging. He wondered how Prabhudas was able to manage a night shift, get so little sleep in the morning and still be that sharp.

By the time he got the front door, it was 7:30pm. His family was in the living room watching their favourite soap, he didn't have the energy to join them tonight.

"Hi honey, how are you? You look so tired. You have also been coming in quite late these days, are you fine honey?"

"I am fine mum, just finding what I love I guess."

His answer sounded a bit confusing to his mum.

"Well done son, that's the way to go boy! Go for what you want! That's how I got your mama. I knew if I didn't get her my life would be miserable; and even now I am holding on to her tightly because she still gets my head to spin. Make sure she is as beautiful and great as your mum."

"Yes papa. Got you loud and clear."

"Is this about who you love Parth or about what you love?"

"Come on mama, is there a difference? There must be something you loved in papa that made you say yes to him isn't it?" Tejas put in.

"Thanks Tj for coming to my rescue."

"Alright son. Take a shower, dinner is ready."

Parth managed to get out of his clothes and sank into an arm chair, in no time he was fast asleep. Subhada came in later to knock him out of sleep and push him to the bathroom. She forced him to eat dinner and kept him awake with stories of how and why she fell in love with his dad. As much Parth yearned for his bed, he knew he dared not sleep. The faster he cooperated with her, the earlier he could reunite with his beloved bed. This bed had been faithful to him all these years, always receiving him into her undiminished bosom. The love they shared was inseparable. The marriage was one he wished to continue even after he married. "… I would love you forever…hold you forever…thank you forever…"

Subhada knew she couldn't force him beyond this. She smiled as she saw her son doze off while she was still speaking. Somehow a sense of pride welled up in her heart, something had changed in him, she could tell. He seemed more decisive, more confident and more energetic. As she walked him to the room, he was sleep talking. She tucked him, checked on Tejas and closed the door behind her.

*   *   *

Parth opened his eyes for the first time at about 8am, but he turned to the other side of the bed and drifted off again.

"Hi Krisha what are you doing here?"

"I came to say hi. We haven't seen each other in days."

"Sorry I traveled to the moon. I saw Ashwini there and we had a good time. She didn't want me to leave and kept me indoors for months, but I loved it though."

"But you promised to visit on Sunday at 4pmn and I waited endlessly. I called your line but you didn't pick."

"Krisha, Ashwini is so beautiful, I just can't live without her. If I try to I just might die. Did you know I almost killed myself? But Ashwini saved me and said she would marry me."

"Parth are you sure you know what you are doing? I can't choose for but you should take things easy and don't rush things. And you could have called to say you weren't going to make it. Anyway, I am leaving for the U.S tomorrow, my work here is done and I have been offered a job there."

"Really? Are you truly leaving? You didn't say anything about the U.S all along."

"Yes, my plans changed, and I had better leave before your Ashwini comes."

"Parth!!! What are you doing with that girl? Didn't I warn you not to ever talk to her again?"

"Ashwini stop! That's my car don't destroy it. I haven't even fully paid for it. Krisha run!!!"

"Don't worry about me Parth. I can take care of myself. Be careful and take care of you. Bye Parth"

"See what you have done! Krisha has left."

"Well I haven't started! I am pulling down this place!"

"Stop it! That's the office…noooo!!!!!"

Subhada rushes in, "Are you fine son? Was it a bad dream? Maybe it was high time you got up, you have had quite enough sleep."

Parth wondered what kind of nonsensical dream he had. He had seen Ashwini destroying the showroom. They had traveled to the moon. He had missed the Sunday appointment with Krish, whom he had called "Krisha" throughout the episode—quite unlike him.

"Besides how did I even get to this bed mum? The last I remember, I was with you in the living room. This dream I had made no sense at all, it was all incoherent."

"It could be the state of your mind. You were really tired last night and even sleep talked when I walked you to your bed."

It was 10:00am, Parth felt lazy. He felt like staying in bed and whiling away some more time. Then he remembered he had an outing later in the day with Krisha. He felt a new surge of excitement. Being alone with her would give him an opportunity to see if she felt anything for him. He had been fascinated at her level of confidence and wondered where it all came from. She didn't seem fazed by anything and she looked like she could really take care of herself.

He kept pondering… "But she looks like she wants something…like she is in search for something. Hmmmmnnn . . . but Krish also seems experienced…that must be it, she is experienced!"

Parth suddenly felt embarrassed, was she reading him like a book already? Was she just checking him out?

"But why would she want to celebrate with me? Could it be…that she has no friends? And the way she asked me over seemed too easy…could she have fallen for me too? Is she trying to make it easy for me?"

Parth suddenly remembered a dream where she had said something about the way they looked at each other—he concluded "…there is more going on here…"

His phone beeped…Prabhudas was calling. "Hello Prabhu, good morning. Are you up already?"

"As ever son, I am always awake. What are your plans this morning?"

"Nothing much, will just relax a bit and prepare for the week. I also have an invite from Krish for 4pm at her place", he giggled.

"Yeah, you both are walking the Path. Don't forget to keep the main thing the main thing."

"What could that be Prabhu?"

"Love…look out for it. That's where the magic of life is. Knowing your god loves you, that you ought to show love to those around you, and that you are to find what and who you love. It is that simple."

"Prabhu I admit it's been magical ever since I took hold of your advice. I mean look at how I felt at Pride

Cars Showroom yesterday, but not everyone can be loved Prabhu. Some people are just cruel."

"Love is a liquid spiritual force, and spirituality implies equanimity. Look upon things with an equal eye and you will find that the love for truth and humanity will help you defeat evil. But you can't be entrusted with such victory if you are biased against people no matter your perception of them. Judge things based on their merit and your judgment will be fair no matter how severe it is."

"What about antecedence? Shouldn't we judge by antecedence?"

"Antecedence should warn and caution you, but the person you met yesterday may be different from who you meet today. Remain cautious and also open. But if there is the pull of love, then always act on love."

"Wow…I am dumbfounded."

"Don't ever allow hate rule you Parth, it will cloud your judgment. Instead allow sound judgment rule you and you will be just in your approach. I was thinking you might still want to see the showroom again? Besides you said there seemed to be vacancies, shouldn't we find out about them?"

"Yes, I would love to. That's true I didn't quite think of finding that out". Parth had to be careful with what he said since he was home; he didn't want to arouse any suspicion.

"I know you can't speak much since you are home, what do you say we meet there in 40 minutes?"

When Parth walked into the showroom at 11:10am, he met Prabhudas waiting for him at the entrance. They exchanged pleasantries. They walked through some of the aisles Parth had seen yesterday as Parth talked about the cars with excitement. There are other parts of the showroom Parth had not seen the day before because of the time constraint. He also saw other aspects of the complex, read through their brochures, saw the slots available which dampened his excitement a bit as they checked through other amazing facilities in the showroom complex. Parth was getting quite bothered.

"It's almost 3 PM son. It's almost 4 hours now since we started moving round the showroom."

"Oh shit. I am so sorry. I should not have done this again. I just forgot that you had other things to do and just enjoyed your being there with me."

"Son, I'm always there with you. But did you notice that the time passed by and you had no clue about it?"

"Yes. I mean four hours? I thought it was like five minutes."

"Let's get a cab. You don't want to be late for your appointment with Krisha."

As the cab man joined the major road, Prabudas asked "So what do you think about the showroom?"

"Oh it's so great. It's fun to be there, I felt like never coming out."

"Ok that's good. Do you remember what I said about love?"

"What?"

"You remember…that part about Love and the object of your love?"

"Yea…when you feel glued to the object of your love, you forget all your pain, and you are just caught up in that moment."

"Isn't that what happened?"

"Huh?…Truly I was glued"

Parth was perplexed. He felt like a current had flown through his mind yet again. He was thinking of how immersed he had been in the showroom with the cars and customers flowing in, and how he did not even remember to have lunch. Even now he was just so desperate to get back into the showroom. But he had seen the advertisement for the positions available…it bothered him. But he asked Prabhudas instead…

"So you think I've found my love?"

"Don't you think so? Don't you think you'll be able visit the showroom every morning with a spring in your steps? Getting out of bed with excitement and spending quality time on the job without even noticing? You forgot your pain for a while."

"Yes. I feel I can actually visit the showroom every day..." Parth muttered halfway with a question in his eyes.

"But... what?"

"How can I possibly do this? I would go bankrupt one day and we will have to beg."

"Well...you don't have to."

"How? They want Customer Service Professionals at Rs. 8,000 per month, with uncertain incentives from happy customers."

"Yes I saw that too."

"I know it's a job opening, but with only Rs. 8,000 per month, how do I survive? It's only one third of what I was getting at the previous job."

"From which you were fired because you didn't love it and hence you couldn't do it."

"Yes, but only 8,000?"

"Do you remember what I said about success?"

"Yes. It's the love with few more elements."

"Yes. That's what I'm getting at. Son, do you want to be successful or not?"

"Yes I want to, I am just confused on how I can be successful living on Rs. 8,000 per month."

"You're gradually letting the ego come into your head again."

"Do you want to be someone successful? Or do you want to give up on your chance for success just because of your ego?"

Parth wanted to hear where this was going.

"The first of those elements is finding a profession you love."

"Now that I have, how do I find success?"

"What do you remember from Sachin Tendulkar, Amitabh Bachhan, and the Singers. How do you think they began?"

"No idea."

"They began by taking the first step. That's how to begin. Choose a job you love. A job that you have some strong connection to."

"Like who?"

"Like Sachin Tendulkar, who first played in local matches and trained hard even when the monetary rewards were next to nothing or non-existent. He did not start playing cricket at the international level from day one. He began small."

"and..?"

"And Amitabh Bachhan started acting in dramas and stage shows as a side hero. He did not get a big role overnight."

"So…is that it?" Parth was getting quite curious. He was at a major crossroad. He felt like something great was going to unfold, yet he also felt there were great uncertainties.

"How do you think I can take the first step Prabhudas?"

"Let's find out tomorrow morning. What do you say we come back tomorrow?"

Parth seemed unsure; he had an uncertain look on his face.

"Listen to your heart. It's telling you what to do. Don't listen to your ego. Don't listen to the noise. Do you have faith in me?"

Parth was amazed by the question and the sudden brightness he felt radiate out of Prabhudas's eyes as he asked. He felt a strange peace, confidence and strength.

"And this is the major turning to Krisha's street; maybe hanging out with her will also help rejuvenate your dreams."

Parth now had a smile back on his face. "Yes. I certainly want us to take a closer look tomorrow at the showroom deal", he said.

"Think about it and let's see if we can make it for 8am. I have to go now, I have work to do."

"I doubt that they open the showroom at that time."

"Never mind, we'll help them open it when they do." Prabhudas said with a smile.

"Ok, tomorrow at 8 in the morning then."

Prabhudas left as Parth took the major turning off the business district towards Krisha's house. He was excited that he had found someone interesting to share time with. He had also found something he loved. Something he could jump out of his bed to do unlike having to call people to persuade them to take a loan. His communication skills will be put to better use talking about something he loved.

But on the other hand Prabhudas had asked him to take a job that was going to pay him one third of what he earned on the previous job from which he was fired. Parth kept thinking.

He remembered how the other day, the kids were playing in the scorching heat and were still happy. He remembered Prabhudas saying Sachin Tendulkar, who is now very rich and successful, once used to play like that. "He kept playing and success came to him. Now he is so rich", he thought to himself.

"When I took the job at Fast Loan, it was an offering that was nearly half or one third of what my other friends at college got, now it looks like I have to choose something that pays me nearly one tenth of what my other friends are earning? How does that even sound? How will it work? My parents will be stoned if they get wind of this."

"But I think I should take it easy…these were the kinds of thoughts that caused me to go for the suicide jump just a couple of days back…To say the least Parth, don't you just love it back there at the car showroom? At least you'll be happy, even though you don't know how you possibly end up successful."

Suddenly Parth remembered the words from Prabhudas, his newly found friend, who had said there were a few more elements in addition to love that were required to be successful.

"Let's cut the crap. I'll just do what Prabhudas says. Today I'm alive just because of him."

He was now looking at the number on the fence across from where he stood. He was on the wrong side of the street. He crossed over and there it was, he was standing right in front of her compound.

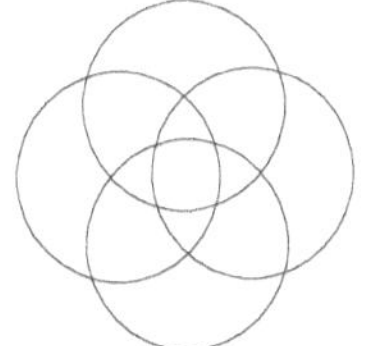

Chapter Seven

Subhada knew something was wrong; she just couldn't lay her hands on it. Tejas had gone to the library for some old references for his school work. He wouldn't be back till late afternoon. Besides he was leaving for school soon. She had thought that since they stayed together he might have noticed anything off about his brother, but she had made up her mind late.

"Sweetheart, haven't you noticed there is something odd about Parth? He is acting a bit strange."

"That's because he is in love, a man in love acts strange. Besides I haven't noticed anything overly odd about him. Why do you ask?" Abhay questioned.

"There has been something odd about his behaviour in the last few days."

"He is probably scared. He wants to be sure before bringing her home. Trust me my love, we men go through a lot to ensure we get it right. I am sure he will come around. Or better still we could make him feel more comfortable to talk about it. He also needs to know it is not a do or die affair? He will find love at the right time, just the same way I found you my darling."

"I want to believe you sweetheart, but I just have this feeling there is more to it than love. I was excited too when I saw the text he sent to her, but Parth seems a little distracted…"

"You saw a text? Really? How come you didn't tell me? That's great honey! We should celebrate! That's his new distraction. It explains why he comes home late."

"What if it's a cover?"

"What do you mean a cover? Are you saying he isn't in love?"

"Well Parth looks like he is in love…but he also looks disturbed…he seems lost. I can feel it. He avoids eye contact, fills up his time with activities, and is hardly around. He wants to avoid questions or moments that could compromise his worries or secrets. I just feel absent in his life."

"Was there ever a time you didn't feel absent honey?" Abhay giggled "Aaahhhh… Subhada eee-aasyyy…darling…easy. You see I never subscribed to you spying on our children, but at some point I conceded when I saw what it did to you when you felt shut out. But these boys have always loved you honey and they open up to you. You think they are only just discovering that you spy on them? But they know it's a mother's love, so they deliberately look the other way."

"That also means, they can choose whatever clues they prefer to leave and extinguish whatever they do not want me to find. And they have successfully done that for years now. Tell me, how long have they known I have been spying on them my sweet traitor of a husband? Why did you tell them?"

"Believe me I have never lied to you honey. I didn't tell them anything…they discovered themselves."

"Well how did you know?

"I know because they told me and we joked about it. But they told me they knew it was a mother's love and that they will never hurt you. Our boys adore you Subhada."

"And you say you have never lied to me? You never told me they knew all along! I feel like squeezing the hell out of you!"

"I never lied honey, I only didn't tell you. I also wanted you to keep filling me in on your findings. At some point it also helped me know a bit more."

"Well there you go love. By not telling me the truth you lied. You pretended. You deceived me."

"Oh my God! You mean I committed all those crimes? Oh my Subhada please forgive me, I…I…was only trying to protect you…and I also wanted to be on the lookout for our boys too. I am so sorry."

Abhay strode to where she stood looking out the window. He held her gently by the shoulders as he gently kissed the side of her neck from behind and drew her into his embrace. He gently wrapped his hands around her tummy. She turned round and hugged him tightly. She couldn't resist the magic in his touch even after twenty-two years of marriage. He had been a hardworker. He had stood by her and the family all these years, even when the doctors had cautioned her about exerting herself too much.

They had both come from very poor families, but her situation at the time they met was worse. Abhay's parents had worked hard to send their three children to school, but when it got too hard they had pushed Abhay through college while they saw the older of the two girls through secondary school. The younger girl had to wait.

After Abhay graduated from his Diploma pro-gramme and secured a job with the Ministry of Consumer Affairs, Food Protection and Distribution, he had taken it upon himself to help their parents in getting the two girls to complete their training at the teachers college—it was why he married at twenty-eight. Both girls had been so close that they literally fell in love with the same things—the only difference was they had fallen in love with different men. All three now helped to support their parents back in their small town, while they had all married and now lived in different cities.

Subhada didn't have it that easy. Her father had been reckless. Her mother had sworn that she was so engrossed in helping her own family that she didn't mingle much. She married late at twenty-six, quite late for a lady who had little formal education. She had married out of desperation. Her real lover had been frustrated years back by her attitude. But her new lover and husband soon revealed himself to be unfaithful and one who didn't care much. He had barely stayed for their honeymoon before going for the next wild party. She married him because he had the means, but he married her because he saw she was naïve, beautiful and desperate.

Her mother had wept for the first five years of the marriage due to her husband's escapades, until he got framed by a rival gang in a drug bust. He was accused of being a conspirator in the murder of a famous politician in the province. He had hired an expensive lawyer who helped sway the court to commute the conviction to manslaughter. Her husband was sentenced to life imprisonment. She had to move the children to Mumbai in order to shield them from the shame and wrath of those who still sought vengeance—they wanted blood. Their life had been hard and their mother after twelve years of toiling had fallen sick. Subhada had been supportive in raising her younger sisters, seeing them through vocational school. She couldn't afford their college education.

She however decided she would marry earlier than her mother if she found a good man. Abhay came into her life and had blown her away with his indescribable heart, dignity, and sense of family life. When they married, she was twenty-two. They have been happy ever since. Despite the meagre resources, when Subhada's health concerns started, Abhay had helped her support her ailing mother, and also her father who had been pardoned after serving twenty-five years of his prison term.

Subhada still ran the business small scale and relied on hired hands, but the trade was waning in the fast growing urban life of Mumbai, and profit was little. They had moved into their present house to minimize the cost of rent, service the college loans, and build their retirement home in the outskirts of the city.

"Sweetheart could it be that we are pressuring our children too much? I feel like they are burdened…so they feel they want to protect us…I think that's what it is honey. But it shouldn't be that way, they are still our boys and we should be the one protecting them. Honey we need to talk to our boys, they need us now."

Abhay nodded as he reflected deeply on what Subhada had said, he too could see she was right. They had to do something before the boys messed their lives up. And there were two things he could readily identify that really shook young adults—pursuing a career and finding love. He had become happy because he had pursued his love to protect people and the country from exploitative and greedy business men.

This was why he had joined the Ministry. It was his own form of activism. He had only taken the offer of early retirement handed to him when juniors he was clearly better than were being promoted ahead of him. At first he had not bothered, but when the politics became too dirty and the purpose of the Ministry was being undermined, he took the offer graciously. He would complete the house after Tejas completed college.

"You are right honey, we need to talk to the boys about making important life choices. Let's look out for a good time before Tj returns to school."

*   *   *

"Hi Parth, I am elated to see you. Just a minute." Krisha came out of the house to open the gate and walk him in.

Krisha couldn't believe her eyes. She saw how his brown eyes were set in the clear whiteness of his sclera. She saw the sparkle of innocence, sincerity and the myriad of questions all wrapped up in it. The certainty he lacked in his eyes, he seemed to have gained in the moderate build of his body. He had his way with words and he portrayed the image of one who had a heritage he was proud of and wanted to protect.

Parth could see how smooth Krisha's skin was, her legs looked more beautiful in her beautiful shorts and she had an ease about her that put him at ease.

"Please come in, welcome to my humble abode."

"There is nothing humble about this place Krish, it's luxurious. You should try come around my place sometime and see what humble means. The fact that our compound is still kind of one of the best in the area should also give you an idea of what it is compared to your posh street."

"Parth gosh…you have your way with words. Did you just de-market and re-market your place just now? God! you are good Parth. You look good too. Fresh kid." She smiled.

"And you look out of this world. Do you know how many guys will kill just to come this close to a beauty goddess and dashing career woman? Krisha trust me, those guys have bells ringing in their heads each time you show up."

"What guys? Naaaahhh…I can assure you Parth, those guys you are talking about won't even allow the bells ring, and if at all they did there will be more appetizing reasons."

"Wow? More appetizing reasons than a lifetime of endless wonders being with you? You must really know a lot of dumb guys—eh…sorry…I called them dumb."

"Well maybe not all of them are after all, considering there is a new kith in the kin who seems to have more magic in his words than these ears have heard", she laughed.

"I just might take you up on that you know, I could push the guy to step up if I discover who he is".

Krisha couldn't hold her laughter when she saw how he wriggled himself out of that. She thought she had pinned him.

"Parth your dribble is amazing. I have never seen this part of you."

"Me too Krish, I surprise myself these days. You and Prabhudas seem to just make me a different person, and I am enjoying it".

She enjoyed the way they teased at each other. Prabhudas really seems to have had such an impact on him in such a short time as his words suggested. Perhaps she would get to know more about Prabhudas today.

"So you care to join me in the kitchen while I serve out lunch."

"I am starving, was so caught up in the show-room, I didn't even realize so much time had passed."

"Oh really?"

"Yeah, Prabhudas put me up to it and he suffered more than you did", he smiled.

"I didn't suffer Parth, it was fun. I was just happy to see you absorbed in something you really loved. I know how I can be with work sometimes, and funny enough Prabhudas has got me thinking a lot too. Those lines he dropped at the resort have given me real food for thought and I have started making serious plans based on those insights."

"Wow, that's really amazing and relieving, because I was almost beginning to feel the whole things was weird. It just felt as though someone monitoring me sent him particularly to me. It's good to know I am not alone. Truly relieving."

"Well don't feel so relieved, It may not mean he didn't come specifically for you. You never can tell. Maybe I am benefitting because of you."

"Oh Krish please you are beginning to freak me out. I know I really prayed a lot of late and I don't rule out that this could be some intervention arranged for my good; but when you say he came specifically for me, that sounds like he is some form of special being, and that freaks me out I think."

"You are lucky to have such a luxury to think of freaking out. With my background, I will be glad to have god or any special being that close to me."

Parth looked her in the eyes and saw her strength and determination. Could there be more to her than he had known, and why did his heart keep beating at such speed since he came into the house? He feared she might notice. As Parth looked into her eyes, he felt electrified and hypnotized—"Is she for real?" He was searching for answers.

Krisha couldn't believe that Parth was staring at her so unabashedly. The tenderness in his eyes was weakening her defenses and making her heart lurch with a mixture of reactions. She couldn't afford to cry in his presence, she got up and dashed to the kitchen.

"Krish, are you okay?"

"Yes I am fine, I just want to get something in the kitchen, just give me a few minutes."

Parth could swear he had seen tears forming in her eyes, what had he done? "Why was I staring at her like that? Did I embarrass her or remind her of something? Why do I always mess things up?"

He thought he heard some quiet sniffs in the kitchen, he felt that whatever he had done he had to right the wrong. He walked to the kitchen and saw Krisha dabbing her eyes with a handkerchief, she had been crying. He felt so sorry, walked up to her and stayed by her side.

"I am sorry, I didn't mean to embarrass you or trigger any memories."

"No Parth, you have done nothing wrong. If anything you just gave me hope, you just made my whole stay in Mumbai these past two years worth it. I feel human again and accepted. I was happy when I got the breakthrough with the investors, but seeing that tenderness and sincerity in your eyes look upon me beyond the quest for some sort of personal achievement broke me. I felt human again after over two years".

As she spoke, the tears trickled down again, and soon they flowed freely and she really began to sob.

Parth didn't know what to do, he felt so overwhelmed with compassion that he just wanted to hold her in his arms. He just couldn't take it anymore. He reached out to her and patted her gently on the shoulders. As she cried, she began to cough. Parth quickly got her some water, and started rubbed her back until the coughing stopped. He then embraced her and told her "All will be well Krish. I promise. You are a not in this alone Krish".

As he spoke, she could feel the gentle and firm vocal vibrations through his chest, she didn't want to leave, and Parth held on to her. Suddenly she felt tired and wanted to sit.

"Could we sit in the living room, I want to tell you why I came to Mumbai."

She told him about why she had dropped her surname so she could earn her way through the market by merit. She had always loved the arts and had paintings of her own.

"Dad liked it. He was proud that I had an interest in the arts and that I was also good with the brush. He always said I won't just be a collector, but will also be a creator. I was always elated that he was proud of me, or so I thought. My older brother was good with arithmetic and numbers. He also knew how to drive a good bargain. He studied Business Management and got an MBA. Dad wanted the same for me, but I was drawn to the arts. He said drawing was a talent and not something to learn in school, but I needed to learn how to handle business. That was when I knew that the plan all along was for me to join his big company."

Krish explained how she studied Business Management and got caught up in the company politics with her two other brothers. Everyone that came into her life saw her as a means to an end—including her suitors.

She had fought her way through to head the arts, artifacts and collections arm of the empire after winning many deals, but subsequently her novel ideas were turned down by her dad, because according to him they were "more charitable than profitable". She had wanted to elevate the arts to a new level.

The stroke that broke the Carmel's back was when she overheard the conversation between her dad and her Ex—she couldn't believe the man she loved so much had other motives. She packed her things and left the house and had never been back in over two years.

"I want to make paintings more appreciated and create a culture where more people want it. Prabhudas' thoughts are showing me that beyond finding what I love and becoming good at it, my target market must be willing to pay for it. That's where I am now, and I am trying to conduct surveys to define my target market."

Parth was amazed at all he had heard, he told Krisha again how inspiring she was to him in carriage and intelligence, and now he seemed hypnotized by her story. She had managed life so well.

"I almost committed suicide some days ago, that's how I met Prabhudas. He saved my life. Actually he brought me back to life".

"What???" Krisha could hardly believe her ears. She listened with keen interest.

Parth told her the entire story. Told her about his family, his challenges in college, job hunting, the Loan Company and Ashwini. They had been together for two and a half hours when Krisha remembered she had wanted to show him the car. They went to the garage and as soon as Parth saw it he mentioned the name of the car, the brand, model, year and features. He was wowed.

"Parth, I am driving you home and there is no going back on that."

"But it's late Krish"

"Nope it isn't. I insist"

*   *   *

As Parth unbuckled his seatbelt he said a hearty "thank you"

Krisha instead hugged him and thanked him for making her human again.

"Parth, you are my guardian angel, you just changed my life. I have not felt this light in over two years. Prabhudas may have saved your life, but you just saved mine and I will forever be grateful."

Parth was mildly embarrassed. He didn't know what to think and he felt touched. He thought to himself "She must really feel alone, and to have come out openly like that takes courage, I shouldn't take that for granted. I must treat her right. This feels different from Ashwini…but even if it's not, I want to be her friend."

For a moment Krisha thought she had blown it all. "Have I been too forward?" she asked herself.

She had really fought back tears while they rode down to Parth's place as she thought about the lonely journey back to her apartment and her world after she dropped Parth.

"All alone again…into my fake world, with fake people, who are only as real as what they can get in return…Maybe I was too quick to say what I just said to Parth, I have only just met him. But it's the truth…" She was deep in thought.

She had to break the sudden silence between them.

"Are you alright Parth?"

Parth broke out of his thoughts and held a wide grin

"Yep, I am good Krish, just that what I wanted to choose my words carefully. I just want you to know I will always stand by you with all I can muster at any time. I can promise you that, with all my heart. You are a good woman and I am privileged to be this close."

Krish felt her heart starting to beat loudly, she was afraid Parth would notice. They hugged again before he stepped out of the car. They waved at each other as she drove off.

When Parth entered the house, his mother had tears in her eyes. Once again she had positioned herself at the window and had practically seen her son fall in love. She couldn't contain her joy.

*   *   *

It was now the fourth morning in a row that Prath had gotten out of bed full of excitement. He was not sure whether he was going to accept the newest idea put forward by Prabhudas but he was excited to visit the showroom yet again.

He also thought about Krish and his heart swelled with waves of joy pouring over him like the ocean at the shore. He prepared for the showroom.

"You're before time again."

"Yea. I told you we can help them open the store… haha."

By 8am, the store opened for business, and Prabhudas and Parth entered the complex.

As they headed into the main area Parth called Prabhudas' attention to an ensuing quarrel between a customer and a customer service representative. It was about one of the cars and a deal.

He wanted to intervene. Prabhudas said "Every problem has its opportunities, it's your call Parth, go and fix them".

"You said my car would have this feature. You've cheated me", blurted the customer.

"No sir I never said so. If you want that feature, it is the upper variant and you will have to cancel your old booking and do a new booking, that's what I am saying."

Parth watched them for a while and listened, after understanding the problem he stepped in.

"Sir I think the same booking you made can accommodate the feature you desire. All you will have to do is to pay a token of Rs. 5,000 more and that part can be custom fitted into the car. Both this version and upper version have the same engine assemblage which allows for the inclusion of the component. The only difference is that the component you crave for was invented during the upgrade to the new model, but it is a fitting you can still have. So it can be done for you. They have the original parts here, just pay the token and you are good. Though, I must say that the new model has other features different from this one."

"I just want that particular feature, the rest is fine! I'm fine with it if you can fix it."

Vinod, the customer service rep, looked at Parth almost as if he had saved his life. He then asked Parth "Can we actually do that?"

"Yes. Go through the manual and the warranty package, it's all covered. I have read it online."

"Eh…how did you know?… I never knew there was a manual for this. We were just given a brochure."

"All cars come with manuals and they publish them on their website online when they launch the car."

Suddenly the quarrel got converted into a productive conversation. The customer was now only talking to Parth and had moved away from Vinod. He was impressed with Parth's knowledge and was asking him more questions.

After the conversation, the customer walked out happily from the store after paying for the additional component. Parth had tears in his eyes as he started running towards Prabhudas.

"I've decided. I'm doing it. I'm applying for this job. I know from the inside that I can do it every day."

"Good. Why don't you apply then?"

"I think there will be a cyber cafe nearby. I will make a print out of my résumé and personally give it to someone in the HR here."

"Great. Let's do that."

They were able to find a cybercafe where Parth made a print out of his résumé. This time as he walked into the showroom, he moved towards the elevators. The administrative office was on the first floor.

"I want to apply for the customer service executive opening. Can you please guide me to who I should talk to?" Parth asked an office staff that was sitting in a cubicle.

"Straight into that Cabin. She is Deepa, the HR Manager."

*   *   *

Deepa was taking a look at Parth's résumé while Parth sat in front of her with excitement written all over his face. She wondered what made him so excited.

"You seem to be overqualified for the job. Your education can easily land you a job in the technology department here. The package is also good there. Are you sure you want to apply for the customer service job?"

Parth was taken aback. He took a moment to think.

"Yes, I want the customer service job. I cannot sit in front of the computer again to handle technology. I love to be among the cars, with the customers."

She liked his enthusiasm. She was glad to have a staff with a college degree with a background in tech, only that he preferred customer service.

"Ok. Not a problem for me. When can you start?"

"Tomorrow?"

"Okay. That would be good. Please bring along some of these documents in the list here and we'll have your job agreement signed tomorrow."

"Tell me one thing."

"What?"

"Do I have to meet a certain number of sales every month?"

"You don't have to. You see this is a very big show-room and customers come here themselves. You don't have to go anywhere. So you have to handle custom-ers well. That is the only expected performance."

"Okay...great. I'll see you tomorrow." As Parth was turning to leave, someone walked in.

"Wait. Please meet Iqbal, he is the Business Manager who also handles customer service. You will report to him."

After a handshake with Iqbal, Parth went down-stairs to see Prabhudas.

"I can't believe it! I have a job again now. The salary is smaller but it will definitely be fun here every day."

"I'm glad that you have a profession you love."

"So when next do we meet?"

"Now you'll be busy here. Please don't expect me to sit at the chair here every day." Prabhudas said with a smile.

"But whenever you feel like seeing me, I'll be around."

"You will be around?...I don't understand...or do you mean I can call you?"

"Now forget all of that son and just focus on the job at hand. Seems like you were offered something with a better pay, isn't it?"

"Prabhudas, this is a bit weird. Are you actually telling me or asking me? Is there more to you or something?"

"Don't be dramatic, isn't it obvious they need hands here, besides I know quite a couple of things." Prabhudas winked at him.

"Yes. I'm excited about this and I will concentrate on it. I was offered a tech post but I turned it down." Parth replied with a smile.

He saw Prabhudas off and began making his way home.

As Parth headed home, he suddenly realized that things were not bad as he had thought. "...I have a job again which I love, and I'm more patient about wooing my girl...eh well I don't know if she is my girl yet."

Parth also started smiling when he realized how stupid and funny he was to have given up on life so fast.

"...Is all of this for real? Is it really as simple as finding what you love...and finding someone who is also drawn to you? Or was Prabhudas divinely sent to me? It looks quite easy...save that I wish I could earn more and know right away if Krisha shares in this pull towards her. Huuuu... that hug really felt like paradise last night and I could tell her heart was beating quite fast...or was that mine?"

Parth kept thinking of what would have become of him if Prabhudas hadn't shown up. That was the defining moment of his life, his turning point. Today he had a job he loved simply because of Prabhudas' guidance. He still had a lot to learn about life and he was more patient with life now, watching to see what next it would bring his way.

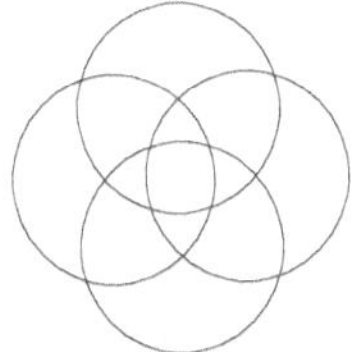

Chapter Eight

As Krisha drove home the other night, she could feel the emotional mixture of warmth and loneliness swirling around her like warm and cold air. She kept thinking of the warmth she felt when she embraced Parth, and the peace and serenity that flooded her mind.

She reminisced "…I doubt there is anything in heaven that could feel better than that…so real, so pure and so warm…Your kind is rare Parth…so rare…" her thoughts trailed off. She could feel the darkness she was driving back into hovering in the air.

All along she had tried to run away from a lot of things in her life. Somewhere deep within her she had felt suffocated and had left New Delhi to find her own path and things had really felt better. But now that Parth had surfaced she had something new to contrast her life with—something she really needed but didn't yet have. She could feel something deep down growing.

She had always done all she did to please her father. He had been strong for them after they lost their mother, and had insisted that they be strong enough to face the world. Krisha was born with a golden spoon in her mouth. Though there was financial freedom, but she had felt choked and bound to keep up with the family tradition and wealth. Instead of taking a course in the arts like she wanted, she had gone to business school, came out as one of the best graduating students, and had joined the family business.

But she couldn't stop drawing, only that she didn't have much confidence in her work. After she was done with her pieces, she stored them away and occupied herself with proving her managerial and business skills. Krisha proved herself within a short time. However she gravitated towards her natural love for the arts and got more deals and income from that angle of the family business—she became one of the most respectable art dealers in India.

Her exploits in pushing competitive ideas and securing profitable deals in the vast family empire spanning media, banking, real estate and hospitality earned her a great deal of respect in the family and among the staff. Politics was also part of the family business because power was important. But something in Krisha still felt odd and covered. She only came alive when she saw a beautiful artwork, worked on new accessions for their collections, or was with her brush and canvas. When corporate politics became unbearable for her, she lobbied her way into oversee the hotels and art dealership segments of the family empire and turned her back on everything else. She didn't budge for anyone, not even her dad.

"...I can see the affection in his eyes and there is surely some chemistry between us. The amazement on his face that day at the café showed he wanted to fall in love and was looking for a partner. Or was I mistaken? Krisha you couldn't just resist luring him could you? Now you have fallen for him...or how else could one know love?" Krisha kept probing into her life as she stared in the mirror that night. She began to feel like she also needed Prabhudas.

Krisha had always known when a guy was interested, she had never been wrong. And she had her own ways of putting them at ease. If she was interested she reciprocated, and if she wasn't she nicely discouraged them while keeping them as friends.

She never allowed things remain ambiguous. They knew where to draw the line even with the friendly atmosphere she encouraged. But here she was trying to work her magic and she seemed ruffled. She couldn't tell who was causing the ambiguity. "Is it me or is it Parth?"

"He has had it rough with the relationship angle, I think he is scared to commit or make a move. Or maybe he needs more time to be sure" she thought to herself.

"But Krisha how could you be so sure?"

This was the first time Krisha was scared of being turned down or that she doubted her own judgment; she simply had never experienced it. Now she had a taste of what Parth must have felt that night when Ashwini turned him down, only that in this case she didn't want to assume things. Parth had made assumptions, and had gotten really bruised for that.

"Like Prabhudas said, if it is love, it would keep growing and it has to be mutual. I think I need to see my own signs too. I need something clearer, something more assuring. I have made two bold moves; I think he needs to make his."

She was going to pipe low until he did, though she hungered for his company every day.

She texted Parth to send her Prabhudas' number as she prepared for bed.

Krisha left the main bulb on that night. She needed the light to keep away the cold darkness trying to cover her mind. She needed to see the events unfolding in her life more clearly.

She prayed for the second time in over two years.

*   *   *

As Krisha woke the following morning, she reminisced on the hangout she had with Parth and Prabhudas, it was one of her best moments in recent times. She had felt good about securing the agreement she had just brokered, and now she had new friends. Maybe life wasn't so lonely after all.

She remembered some of the points Prabhudas had made. He had said

"...If you can trace your passion to people's real needs or something they really want, and catch their attention, then you could as well get them to pay for it...it becomes a viable occupation...something people are willing to pay you for."

"Hi Prabhu good morning"

"Hey princess, great to hear from you!" Prabhudas' voice was full of excitement.

"Today is my day I guess. It's good to hear that beautiful voice of yours. It's been like ages you know?"

"What do you mean ages Prabhu?...its less than 48 hours since we last spoke".

"I bet it's more than that...or at least it feels that way. I could have gotten your number form Parth but I didn't want to distract you both, was hoping you would call. Good to hear from you again."

Krish felt like she and Prabhudas were talking about something else; what did he mean by it's been ages? She was saying one thing, but he seemed to be saying quite a lot of other things. Anyway she got his hint on Parth.

"Same here Prabhu. I have been thinking a lot about your theories on that "*Iki...something*"...I can't remember the name now. But I remember the points though".

"You mean "*Ikigai*"? Yes, you want us to talk about it?"

"Yes Prabhu, I want to know more about how to develop something into a vocation"

"Well I am at your service Krisha, just let me know when you need me".

"Actually I had thought to first find out what's convenient for you".

"Well by Wednesday I will be back to the morning shift and will have the nights to myself".

"What about tomorrow at noon. You would have had time to rest a bit. Besides I wouldn't be going to the office, I want to use the time to straighten out my thoughts on the options before me after meeting with my team today".

"That's great Krisha, tomorrow at noon then. I am on my way to the showroom to meet with Parth"

*　*　*

On the night Parth got the job at the showroom, he knew he needed to tell his family.

"Congrats bro, you now have a job you love and that's what really matters" Tejas said.

Subhada was shocked.

"You mean you left such a tech job to be a show-room attendant? Don't they have better paying posi-tions open for a college graduate at the showroom?"

"Mum, technology isn't my thing. I have strug-gled with it for years. But I feel something about this job, it fills me with life."

"Then you could have studied mechanical engi-neering or marketing, and would have been over-qualified to lead the entire complex!"

Abhay was unusually quiet. He was stunned at was he was hearing and hoping he would wake up from this dream.

"Subhada is that you? are we really awake right now or asleep?"

"Of course Abhay it's me! You never dream during the day honey! You are not like your son. This is real not a dream. He just took a job for high school leavers."

Abhay got up in a frenzy from where he sat and said he was going to sleep at the shrine.

"I don't know what the world is turning into these days. Perhaps we haven't prayed enough, if we sleep at the shrine god will have mercy".

Tejas motioned to his father, "Dad, take it easy. It isn't that bad. God should rest a bit don't you think? He is doing his part already by guiding us. Let's make the most of it."

Abhay got into his room to get his covering and other materials for his worship that night, he seemed serious. As he opened the door to move out, Subhada held on to him crying.

"Stop acting crazy Abhay, if you go who will pacify me?..." she sobbed.

"I just want to ask you one question guys. Do you want me happy? Do you know I almost committed suicide a few days ago?"

"What!!!" Tejas exclaimed.

Subhada stopped crying immediately and rushed to the side of her son. Abhay pinched himself and sat on the sofa close to him.

"Why son? Why would you do that my boy?" Abhay asked in absolute shock. Subhada was still trying to process the words she had just heard.

"Actually I was practically gone. If one of the guards at the "New Gate Tower" hadn't come just in the nick of time, I would probably be dead today."

Subahada couldn't believe her ears, the tears ceased and her eyes became blank.

"I had struggled so hard with this job and yet I couldn't even meet my targets for the day. I was fired. Though they gave me some sort of compensation, that's why it didn't get so obvious."

Subhada spoke, "But I could feel it all along, I knew something was wrong, I just couldn't lay my fingers on it. Subhash's answer was awkward, looking back now I see that he had avoided lying, but he didn't tell me the truth either."

"I didn't want to fail you guys. I know how hard you both have worked to keep this family going and to say the truth I don't have all the answers to the many questions on your minds right now, but I just had to do this. When you have such a close shave with death, you see things differently. They offered me a position in the technology unit, but I turned it down. I don't know how, but I really believe we would get through this."

"Come here boy", Abhay got up and gave Parth a hug.

"I know this is tough for you, but you would get through this son", Abhay consoled him.

"You know, after I saw that beautiful girl last night, I thought that perhaps it was all a love issue all the while—though something still didn't quite settle. But I should have known better because you were avoiding eye contact too. I love you honey and I am always proud of you sweetheart. We just want the best for both of you, but I think we have put you both under too much pressure without knowing it." Subhada said as he planted a kiss on his forehead and rubbed his left cheek.

"Thanks mum", tears were in both Parth and Subhada's eyes as they hugged each other.

Abhay dropped his worship materials, "Don't worry son, we would find a way to sort ourselves out. For now you should shower, eat and catch some fun with us. You have had a long day...and besides you haven't told us enough about this damsel of yours."

"Yeah, maybe I should first tell you I had a crush on someone else for so long that I got obsessed with her. She also rejected my proposal the day before I got fired."

Subhada felt so much sympathy for him. Matters of the heart were delicate issues. "Sweetheart, I am so sorry you had to go through all that alone."

"Well there was this man…I mean the security guard…he has been amazing. His name is Prabhudas. He seems strange but a dependable friend and wise man. He has been my counselor; and then Krisha came along the line… all in one day. It still amazes me."

"You should bring them home son, so we can express our gratitude to both of them."

"Ok, I will invite them against next Sunday afternoon when Prabhudas would be back to his evening shift."

Parth felt relieved. Now he had his family's support. He knew the road ahead still had a lot of uncertainties, but felt a new confidence and sense of control in his life. He felt more alive and more in charge of his life's direction. He decided to spend quality time that night with his family.

Something in him wanted to talk to Krisha, he wanted to celebrate his new job. The time he was spending with his family now was both restorative and reconciliatory, but he also wanted to celebrate.

He texted her.

"I got the job! Celebrate with me tomorrow night please...had to get my family along tonight. What do you say I pick you up to a new spot I just found? Nothing fancy."

Parth would have to break his pocket a bit to pick a cab and pay for refreshments for the outing; but he just wanted it, he really wanted this moment to be perfect.

"Wow!!! Congrats!!! I would love to celebrate with you. What time do I expect you?"

Parth giggled when he saw her message come in, he replied "7:30pm".

"Mum and Dad, I just got another outing with Krisha tomorrow for 7:30pm! Hurray!!! I just hope she likes me."

*   *   *

The following evening as Parth and Krisha celebrated the new job, they laughed, talked and kept looking into each other's eyes throughout their time together. Parth could tell Krisha was really happy for him and was very comfortable around him.

His heart was beating faster than usual. She looked so elegant that evening. Her natural beauty got his mind spinning.

He remembered her smell from the hug of the previous night and he longed for another opportunity to be so close and to be enchanted by her fragrance.

Krisha knew that look, she could suddenly tell at a point that Parth wasn't really hearing her jokes anymore. He was practically boring his eyes into hers, and she held his gaze deliberately. She knew he was fantasizing, she could tell. Perhaps this was the sign she was waiting for.

She gently reached out for his hand to see if it would break him out of it. She was right. He shuddered a bit as though he had been dozing.

"What just happened Parth? You seemed lost. There are no cars here, so what got you off like that this time?"

"You are beautiful. I mean…you are indescribable."

Krisha felt shy, she was caught off-guard. She didn't know what to do. That wasn't the first time he was saying she was beautiful, but this was different.

She remembered what Prabhudas had said to her that Tuesday afternoon about love. It looked so much like it. She felt the union.

*   *   *

Earlier that Tuesday as Krisha picked Prabhudas for their lunch hangout, she noticed that there was a silent glow and radiance about him. She couldn't help but think about some of the observations Parth had made to her.

As they she drove into the premises she said "Parth told me you guys admired this place"

"Yes, it's quite an elegant input the owners have made here. I hear they are shooting for a five star rank."

"Wow I can see that you and Parth talk often. He has hinted you already. Yes it's true, I am close to the manager and they are closing in on a five star rank."

"It wasn't Parth who told me actually, I have my way around town. I know what's going on."

"Wow, that's impressive. You are quite one wise man I have yet met, and you seem to be good with people."

"I have a special connection to people, to humanity. If people would learn to love one another life would be really more colourful. Understanding life would be easier and better."

"Talking about love, Prabhudas I have some tough questions to ask. Like what really is love?"

"Love is like a magnetic pull between two hearts, calling out to each other. The closer they get to each other as they both respond to that pull, the electrified they become. Love responds to the core of who we really are. And like every other living thing, it needs to be nurtured through mutual affection, trust and support. When love is one-sided it will gradually wither or eventually implode."

Krisha was spell-bound. They had sat there in the car park talking about love.

"This is getting interesting Prabhudas, I will keep chewing on those words. Let's go inside, because I want you to tell me your love story. I want to know how you came by this much wisdom."

"Alright, I am all yours Krish."

"Did you just call me Krish? Parth is the one that calls me that?"

"Yeah, that's because I am sure he would have said the same thing."

Krisha was a bit puzzled about what he meant by Parth would have said the same thing. What was Prabhudas driving at?

"Sorry Prabhu, I didn't get that."

He winked at her and said "Never mind my dear, you will figure it out. Trust me."

As they walked toward her favourite corner, she noticed a couple was just leaving. They sat and placed their orders.

"I discovered quite early that I love the brush and canvas. My dad was glad, but he insisted that I needed business acumen and that going to school to learn the arts wasn't a wise option because according to him real artistes are born not made. He felt I already had the talent, there was no point going to learn another course in college about it."

"Your dad is an ambitious man and is steeped in the traditions of elitism."

"You just gave a perfect description Prabhu. As usual, your wisdom hasn't failed you. From the little I have said you were able to decode that much."

"Don't blame me, I have seen and still see quite a lot daily."

"Hmmn, I see. So tell me about "*Ikigai*". I believe there are a lot of people like me who are good artistes, but they aren't allowed to express themselves because the market is still quite narrow. Those who make the big money do so in the international market by selling old works, or those of world renowned artistes. There is an established market internationally, but the local one isn't existent. I got this investment majorly because I showed the investors I understood the international market, but I also want to build the local market."

"You see Krisha, there is a growing middle class in our urban cities and they love beauty, particularly when it reflects an urban sentiment. But artistes who want the patronage of this middle class must find out what will tickle their potential customers. Artistes shouldn't only live in a utopia of their own; they should also mirror the beauty of society back to society in an attractive manner. Your artistic mind and your business training will help you."

"So you are saying we need to train artistes to be able to observe not just their environment, but the psyche of their prospective customers so they can produce for them? Hmmmmnn…so artistes still need training, but we must go beyond the brush and canvass to help them study their market."

"Exactly. But that's just one leg, and that relates to artistes. There is a place for you the business expert. There is a reason for marketing products. It is to help people discover something they need or want and present it in an attractive package so they can make up their minds. You need to creatively market the arts, not just advocate for it. Go from just advocacy to marketing, until it becomes a trend and commodity. That's what '*Ikigai*' is about. Making your passion your mission; and getting people excited or interested enough to pay for it."

"Wow! You could easily lecture at the best universities Prabhu, why stay a security guard?"

"Remember Krisha, *'Ikigai'* means 'the reason for your existence'. It starts with your passion; that is, something you really love to do or that you want to solve. Then next is for you to develop yourself at that thing so that it becomes a profession; that is, it becomes something you are proficient at. After professionalism, you must see yourself deploying your passion and proficiency in a missionary sense; i.e. you must have a goal. For some their goal is to win an election, for others it is to cause a change, and for businesses it is to both make an impact or impression on the market that will create patronage. Define your mission in clear terms.

"I see your point Prabhudas."

"I am not surprised. You are brilliant. There is one more point. To make it an occupation that pays you, it is important to find out how your prospective customers think, what they want, and what they fancy. And then be very innovative about stoking those resident desires in them so they are willing to pay for it. In order words you must be adding value that they appreciate and want. Value addition will strengthen your marketing."

Krisha sat there in awe and amazement. Who was this man? How did he come to know so much? She went to business school and yet life had never been this clear to her. She understood what he was saying. She knew what value addition was and how marketing in itself contributes to that process.

"Prabhudas, who really are you?"

"Well Krisha don't you think that should be a question for another day? I fell in love several years ago and I have been in love ever since with the best nurturer in existence, and we care about our children. That's what we have dedicated our time to and that's why I have been moving around trying to help them in their different cities."

Krisha listened with undivided attention. She could tell Prabhudas was saying a lot more.

"But let me clear your doubts on why I am a security guard here. I am here both to guard and to guide. How do you rate me? Am I good at it?

"You are the best teacher I have ever met Prabhu. You are truly a guide"

By the time they were done, it was 3pm. They strolled to the parking lot together. Krisha insisted on dropping Prabhudas off—wherever he was going. He opted for the office complex. He said he would rest there in one of the rooms till his shift.

As Krisha was about to drive off, he said to her "keep your international market, you will need it."

As she drove home, she knew she had gotten a breakthrough and that she had a lot of thinking, conceptualizing, planning and implementing to do in the days ahead.

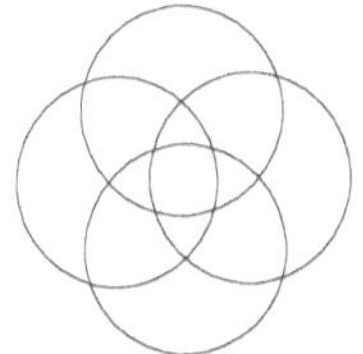

Chapter Nine

It was now two calendar weeks since Parth had signed the contract with the showroom. He also had not seen Prabhudas since the Monday they had both come. Though they had spoken over the phone often, but Parth had gotten so occupied with the job that he would hit straight at the showroom quite early every morning and return late in the evening.

But this morning, Parth was really missing Prabhudas. He decided he was going to have to see him first before going to the showroom. He had to leave early enough.

Parth went to his office building and checked for him at the gate but Prabhudas was not there. He turned towards the security guard he met and asked

"Please where is Prabhudas? He works here as a security guard?"

"Who???" The security guard had a questioning look on his face.

"Turn around Son. I'm right here."

Parth felt relieved as he turned around and he saw Prabhudas in his characteristic bright aura.

"I was missing you. I thought I should see you first today before going to the showroom."

"I told you, I'm always around. Just think of me and I'll be there."

"Yes. So true, you said that and that's why I came."

"So how is it going at the showroom?"

"Oh it's just more fun every day. I didn't even realize that it's been two weeks since I joined them."

"Well. The time to unveil the next element of success will come soon."

"When? Can't you tell me now? I'm so excited to hear it."

"Be patient son. You'll have it when you're ready."

Another week passed by and Parth was now getting the attention of his fellow workmates and the administrative staff at the office. Everyone would refer customers to Parth when they had any doubts.

Many of his colleagues in customer service sought his help when they were stuck in with some question. It was becoming a regular occurrence now to see Parth stand in front of ten to fifteen customers and some of his colleagues—explaining all the features of a car in an astute manner. He also had his way with words. His voice was clear and loud enough to get the attention of a lot of people. It looked like a natural leadership ability which was undiscovered until Parth joined the showroom.

Parth was giving a similar explanation to about twenty customers when Ashutosh, the owner of the store, had come to the showroom for one of his unscheduled visits. He was surprised to see someone that he did not know handle the customers so well. Before the opening of the showroom, Ashutosh had interviewed most of the staff himself but Parth had joined after a month of the showroom's opening.

Ashutosh was impressed.

"Who is the guy over there?" Ashutosh asked the showroom manager.

"Sir, he's Parth. He's new here but everyone's favourite. He knows cars like no one else. He has resolved a lot of our customers' complaints with very simple solutions."

"Really? Can you send him to my cabin when he is done?"

Parth did not know Ashutosh as he had not seen him before. While he was entering Ashutosh's cabin, he knew that he was someone who was very senior as the manager of the showroom himself had conveyed the message to him saying "The boss wants to see you in his cabin."

"Good afternoon sir."

"Come in Boy. I've heard good things about you. I'm the owner of this place."

"Wow! This place is yours?" Parth said in amazement.

"Yes, we are majorly in the real estate business, but we thought of this showroom concept of ourselves."

"If you have any problem or need any help here, contact me on my cell phone directly. Here is my card."

"Thank you sir." Parth was overwhelmed.

When Parth noticed Ashutosh going out of the showroom, he saw that Ashutosh himself owned the latest of the BMW 7 Series Sedan.

*　*　*

After a couple of days, Parth was doing his regular customer presentation session in front of a car.

After the explanations, questions and answers, Parth had the chance to grab a quick lunch. As he was walking away from the cars towards the gate, he was surprised to see Prabhudas in front of him.

"Prabhudas!! You're here. Wow. I am so happy. I'm glad you thought of coming over."

"Yes son. The time has come to unveil the next element of success."

"Wuuhuu! I am excited. Tell me. What is it?"

"Come outside for a while. We'll talk over a walk."

After a few minutes, Parth asked,

"So, what is the next element?"

"It's marketing. The Mass Market Awareness. I have shared a bit of it with Krisha, but hers had more to do with a new market she is trying to open up, so I explained creating a paid occupation closely with mapping out a market to reveal and exploit its existence. If there is no market for your product, you can't get salesmen to sell it."

"Ok. So what is it all about? I know a little bit about marketing, but what is mass market awareness."

"Let me give you an example."

"Remember someone successful. To start with, let it be a popular artiste."

"Asha Bhosale, the singer."

"Yes. So by now you know one thing about her."

"Yes. I know that she loves singing. She can keep signing every day. It's as good as effortless for her."

"Perfect. You learn very fast. But now tell me. If she was the best singer and you didn't know about her, what would happen?"

"She would not be famous."

"Exactly. If she had not taken her singing to every-one, no one would like her. She would have the best voice yet she wouldn't be famous."

"Oh. But how can one just start singing in front of everyone."

"Well son, this is it: I am telling you about the element, it's for you to figure it out how you are going to implement it. Now, let's talk about your favourite cricketer Sachin Tendulkar."

"Yes. He too really loves to play cricket."

"Yes, but had he kept playing cricket somewhere on the street or in his compound would he have been famous?"

Parth shook his head sideways to say no.

"So you are saying that when you love something, you will have to take it to everyone?"

"Not just when you love, but when you have gained sufficient proficiency in the skill."

"Why?"

"Every skill and profession has room for failure. But it's only when one is proficient in it that he can take it to the people on such a level. What would happen if Sachin Tendulkar kept getting out and couldn't score a run?"

"Right...people wouldn't love him as they do."

"Yes, because you can only take it in front of the public when you've gained enough mastery to impress people. When you take it to the people, the stakes are higher and the room for error is very minimal. Likewise, the movie makers who feature the great actors we see only take their movies to the people when they're ready, just like businessmen take their products to the market when they are ready."

"I see. So you think I'm ready to take it to the people? And how should I possibly do that?"

"As I said before son, I've told you the element; you would have to figure out when and how you are going to do it."

"I have to leave now. Just think of me whenever you wish to see me and we'll catch up."

That evening, as Parth was on his way home, he kept thinking over what Prabhudas had taught him. He thought about all those successful people he knew. He learnt the logic that people couldn't be successful if others didn't know them for what they are proficient at. They are successful people because people like them for what they do.

Parth remembered the electronics company baron who manufactured a particular music player. He was a very successful person.

"So people buy his music device because they know about the product and its quality in the first place. Had he not made people aware about what product he had and just kept it in his shelf, no one would know about it—hence, no one would buy."

Things were starting to get clearer in Parth's mind.

"How do I take myself to the people? Will they like me? At least the ones at the showroom like me. Maybe it's worth a chance. Maybe I'm ready."

Over the next few days, Parth kept thinking about how he was going reach out to more people. He started thinking up ideas.

*   *   *

Ever since that night that he took Krisha out to celebrate his new job, they had spoken every day and had gone out every Sunday. He didn't know what came over him that night. He simply lost his ability to say no to what he was feeling. He could see it in her eyes that she loved him. She had never objected to him, had invited him to her house. He remembered how she had run into the kitchen that day with tears in her eyes. The atmosphere had become electrified.

She replied his messages, shared her important moments with him and regularly stole looks at him.

He had caught her severally. And that night as he sat there listening to her, he saw the way her eyes held his gaze, the depth in her words, the shyness that flickered often and the bubble of excitement she was obviously controlling. Parth said to himself "What other signs do I need? She is right here before me, I can see her…I see her…she is mine…she is here…she wants me."

It was then that he felt her tender hand touch him and a bolt of electricity went through his being. In that moment of ecstasy, his heart was pumped with courage and words began to flow out.

It was that night that he told her he loved her. He held on to her hand and asked her if she felt the same way and if they could start a relationship? She blushed, covered her face in shyness and laughed.

"I love you too Parth, I thought you were never going to ask. I was getting scared that I had misjudged what I felt was happening between us. Nothing else will make me more joyful than to spend the rest of my life with you sweetheart. I have spent sleepless nights hoping this moment would come one day."

Parth could not describe the liquid joy that enveloped his entire being and sweetened his tongue. A masculine confidence, sense of mission and clarity took hold of his mind. Somehow he understood better what a family was—a place of security, shelter and support. A place to experience unconditional love, learn about livelihood, and a pillar to lean on. Just like his family where love was deep, lavish and mutual, he knew his future with Krisha held such a promise. His heart beat took on a new rhythm; he could feel Krisha was now part of his destiny.

For another week they met every day. They visited Prabhudas to share the news with him. Parth also invite Krisha to meet his family and they had a nice time. It was a week full of new developments at the show room, new ideas about the gallery project, and new found love and family.

Krisha had traveled the following week to reunite with an old friend of hers. Kiara had been her best friend right from primary school and they had grown and lived in the same neighbourhood. She was also from a well-to-do family. It was Kiara who had shown Krisha that sometimes it was necessary to start out life afresh and embark on a journey to self-discovery.

Kiara had fallen in love with Jairaj towards the end of her second year at college. Kiara was no doubt one of the most beautiful girls on campus. She had dated briefly in high school, but she had wanted to build a future with someone. Jairaj was intelligent, hardworking and also fun-loving. He had the blend of stability and fun that she wanted in a man. He was from a well-to-do family too.

Jairaj was easy-going and fun loving, but he was also a very competitive and ambitious man. He knew how to win a woman's heart though he had no plans to fall in love just yet—he wanted more victories and more fun. Jairaj's family had originally been very poor, and he was born with a front set of protruding teeth that made his classmates make fun of him in primary school. Though he was brilliant, but his esteem began to dampen in his final elementary class. He resumed his junior days in secondary school with low esteem and had become an academically average student.

In those days, Jairaj's family could barely feed, so the question of correcting Jairaj's teeth was out of it. Jairaj's father, Raj, had called the family to a meeting one day to roll out his plan to tackle poverty. He was to smuggle himself to the industrial factories in any of the countries in Europe or North America through one of the ships. They didn't see their dad until the fourth year when he came back with a hard earned savings of $42,000, most of which he invested into running for the state legislative assembly. Jairaj's older brother, Aadrik, had dropped out of school to help his mother support the family during their father's absence.

It was politics that took them out of the woods and Jairaj's father did all to remain popular; and he truly became very popular. He also skillfully aligned with the most powerful blocs within the political space and mentored Aadrik in developing the family's business empire. The result was that the family became prosperous politically and financially. Jairaj had come home one day crying in bitterness about his teeth and the shaming he got in school that day. Raj took him on a walk and by the time they got back, Jairaj saw the world differently. Jairaj was also scheduled for a corrective procedure with the best dentist in India.

In his last two years in secondary school, Jairaj regained his footing academically and won the highest number of medals in sports. He schemed and cunningly got all the girls in the league of the top five to date him before graduation. By the time he got to college, he had bigger plans. He would conquer the field first and then marry the most strategic of them all. He started dating those from the very top of the league from his freshman year. Some well orchestrated issues always ended the relationships before he moved to the next. He also dated simultaneously from across two other leading colleges in the country.

By the time Kiara got into college, he was in his third year. Within her first semester, she was the talk of the campus, and she gave no one a chance. She was good and knew the tricks. In Jaira's final year, something in him wanted to win this final trophy. If others couldn't, he wanted to. When Jairaj saw that Kiara had an eye for him after many subtle show offs, he made his move. She saw he was fun-loving, topped his class and was ambitious. But he was also serious about what he wanted.

In the end they both changed each other. Kaira was his toughest; he almost gave up, but only continued because he couldn't afford to lose. Kaira got him to meet her family, she fell in love with him and became flattered when she realized he had cut-off all other ties with any woman anywhere for a semester. He had flashed all the cards before popping the joker—he proposed marriage. She was shocked.

He captured her heart. He met her family during the holiday. After his final papers, they talked a lot that night. When she talked about marriage, he became withdrawn. She got scared. He told her he was scared about life, he didn't know if he was a good man enough. Her heart softened as she assured him.

They got emotional and made love. She had guarded against it all along, but she had also changed too.

They met every weekend at his place as their emotions ran wild. Something in her got scared, she felt exposed. They had been together for a year and few months when Jairaj couldn't take the monotony anymore, he needed a new challenge. There were hot girls in the political circle and they were more strategic for him. He got busy, they saw less frequently…until she caught him cheating twice. She called it off. He made no move. There she had it—she suddenly realized that was his plan all along.

*   *   *

Krisha was elated to hear her voice again after so many years. She had missed their friendship and Kaira filled her ears with a lot of good things that had now happened. Krisha still remembered the emotionally laden letter Kaira had written her to tell her she was cutting-off to regain her sanity. She assured everyone she wasn't committing suicide and that she needed to be strong so she had to go.

Krisha had now come to see her after such a long time. Krisha also felt this was a good opportunity to make peace with her past and reunite with her own family. She had found her footing and had found love, and she felt whole again.

* * *

Parth was out of his bed and preparing to go to the store. For the past 2 weeks he had been thinking about what he and Prabhudas had talked about.

"Creating Mass Awareness…"

He had discussed it with Krisha and she had also shared what Prabhudas had taught her. Parth kept thinking about it all, looking for the breakthrough idea.

Days at the showroom flew by.

During the staff briefing the day before, Parth had noted a point by their manager when he said

"More people are expected to visit in the future. We're trying our best to make people know that this is the first massive multi-brand car store opened in the city. As people know, they'll choose our store over other ones because this place is a one stop shop for eighteen car brands now."

"What if…I…! Whoo…Eureka!" Parth rejoiced as he hurried out of his house. He reached the Showroom on time and met with his manager.

"Sir is boss Ashutosh expected to come in today?"

"No idea? Anything that you need from him?"

"Well yes, but thank you sir. Let me see."

Parth grabbed a landline phone at the office, took out the business card of Ashutosh from his wallet and dialed the mobile number.

"Hello sir, this is Parth here. I work at the showroom. We met the other day at your cabin."

"Yes I remember. Tell me boy."

"Are you going to be in the office today sir? I have an idea that I want to share."

"Oh great. I will be there for a couple of hours from 11am. Why don't you come and see me by 11.15?"

"Yes. I'll be there for sure sir."

For about two hours, Parth was engrossed in his thoughts about the idea he was going to put forward to Ashutosh. Parth also handled a few customers that had walked in.

At 11:15am he was at Ashutosh's door.

"Come in Boy. Tell me."

"Sir, I was thinking about our core concept for a multi-brand showroom."

"Go on."

"The biggest benefit that we offer to customers is the ability to compare various features between multi-brand cars in the same segment."

"Right."

"So if we have to attract more customers, we have to make more and more people aware about this concept."

"Yes, so what are your ideas?"

"What if every week, we shoot a video on the cars recently launched by the brands, comparing between them? I believe it would delight viewers. The video will be shot in the showroom and we will put the courtesy to the store only."

"How will that help?"

"First, it will be at a low cost to the company to get a videographer. We will afterward upload these videos on social networking sites so that people can share them between themselves. The competitive comparison between cars will attract a lot of attention to the showroom. This will also bring in more customers who love cars who would want to check out these things."

Ashutosh thought for a while. "Wow, this makes sense. But who will speak? I don't want to. I can't speak in front of the camera."

"I will do it. I would love to. I do the same thing here every day, so it's not new for me."

"Okay, bring the videographer and get his payment from the accounts and let me know when the video is ready."

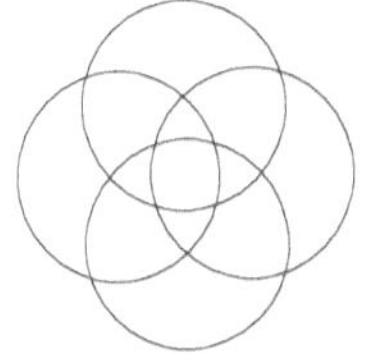

Chapter Ten

"Money is created by value and value is created by our commitment to something we love. If you don't love something, you can't give it your all; hence value will not be created. Money is created as a byproduct of value."

*   *   *

"Kiara it's so good to set my eyes on you again, look at you…you are really looking good."

"It's been tough Krisha, but you know after Jairaj did what he did, I felt like I was going to die. How I managed to write my final exams was a miracle. I didn't want people to see me collapse, so I kept pushing. I just felt fooled. I mean how did I not see through it?"

"Yeah I noticed you were disturbed, and I tried to come around. But I could tell you were so fragile on the inside, even though remained very friendly and accommodating. So I didn't want to break that too. I am sorry if I wasn't there for you as I should. In the last one year I have known what loneliness feels like and it must have been terrible what you went through."

"Krisha you were there for me. Apart from my family, your friendship was perhaps the only other real thing I knew I couldn't doubt. We schooled in different places but you made out time to come see me. If not for you I may have dropped out of college in my finals. You got my letter didn't you? And the ones I started sending some two years back?

"I got your first letter Kiara, and it was consoling. I haven't been here in the last two years so I didn't get the rest. Only I wished you allowed me be there for you. You didn't have to go through it alone…it hurt me so badly to see you cut-off the support system you had here…it felt like you wanted to own the pain alone. We are family Kiara…and family stands by their own."

Kiara had tears in her eyes.

"Krisha I am so sorry I hurt your feelings. I know it must have felt selfish, but I actually did it because I was scared of how flat I might fall. I saw your struggle at home to prove yourself, I couldn't afford to ruin your life; you needed to concentrate. That's why I left you a letter that would put you at ease."

Krisha sniffed as tears flowed down. They hugged each other. It had been over five years now.

"I joined the family business and was there for three years…", she said in between sniffs,

"…until I felt choked and left for Mumbai. I have been there for over two years now. I really missed you. At first when I was here I coped because it was new and I traveled a lot, but after two years I got tired and there was no one to talk to. Fake relationships happened in between and one morning I said I had taken enough and moved. Just like you."

"You have had some tough time yourself Krisha. So how has it been? Were you able to settle down a bit and find something worthwhile?"

"Well let's talk about you first. How have you been, how are you now?"

"I was getting drunk every night for the first week. I ended up in a gutter one night and slept there until a woman recognized it was a person lying in the filth and rescued me. I couldn't allow the shame. I left her place that afternoon while she was still at work and I had regained my composure. I left some good money behind to compensate her kindness. I was damaged and full of revenge. I wanted to have my pound of flesh for what Jairaj did. I joined a martial arts group."

"I hope you didn't do anything stupid Kiara? Revenge consumes."

"I wanted to kill Jairaj. That was the plan. But my martial instructor saw I was a troubled soul and helped me. I became soft enough to drop out of the classes. I also met this counselor, she is very good. I was attracted by the ease with which she displayed her elocution at a conference on the complexities of human psyche. Yet I could tell she was happy. I spied on her for weeks only to discover she had a good home despite her flourishing career. Such perfection beat my thoughts."

"Wow…I can imagine I would have felt the same way".

"I started having sessions with her and after two years I could say I had healed. But I wasn't only healed, I was refocused. I started out to find a career path and today, after three years in human resource management, I am a HR Manager at a multinational. Just got the appointment two weeks ago and all necessary hand-over notes have been done. I asked for a week before I resume fully."

"Wow, I always knew you had it in you Kiara. Yours is a truly fascinating and touching story. I have always admired your strength. I learnt how to blend natural confidence, strength and friendliness from you. You were like my role model you know. And now it looks like we have both come out good in the end."

"Well I would like to hear your story Krisha."

"I just secured a huge deal with some investors for an arts gallery after more than two years of doing in-house consulting in a joint venture I entered into with a big firm in Mumbai. They relate with big international agencies, NGOs, multinationals and big businesses from around the world on hidden arti-facts, articles, items, sites and resources of value. I also helped with PR. There is stuff happening in this world girl."

"Yes Krisha, there is a lot of potential and wealth in hidden places."

"Now there is this middle aged wise man I met, his name is Prabhudas. He has been an awesome life guardian I must say. So things have really been look-ing up in Mumbai. I also...ehm...met...this..cha.. aaarming guy you know..."

"Wow!!!! Kiara screamed and hugged her tightly. "Are you for real?"

"Yes, it's for real Kiara. Life has taken on a new meaning for me. It's like the chaos of the world just stopped for me in that moment he declared his love for me. …And…ever since the chaos has remained distant. I see and hear it all, but I feel like I am not alone anymore in this world to face life with all the good ups and bad downs it brings."

"I am so happy for you honey, how were you able to do it? I mean a guy has been trailing me of late, but I must say I am too proud to admit that I am scared. I can't seem to trust my judgment anymore after it failed me once. I know I have healed, but you know what they say, once bitten, twice shy."

"Well I was bitten more than once Kiara, but I just knew this one was it. Don't worry girl I got you. I will be your teacher on this one."

They both laughed heartily and talked about many other things.

*   *   *

It was 9 O' Clock in the morning and a team of three young boys were bringing large bags into the Showroom.

Parth was up early and had borrowed his father's blazer for the day.

He had also found a good videographer from his network of friends.

"We'll shoot two videos. For the newly launched electric car and the D segment cars which were launched this week by three auto makers. I want us to show the rapid growth in this industry."

Parth was explaining to the videographer who was also directing his crew to set up the lights.

All members of staff at the showroom were gathering to see the setup. Parth had been at the showroom only for only a month and some weeks, yet the energy that he had brought into the place was contagious and well appreciated by everyone. Parth was the problem solver. He had such a vast and detailed understanding of every car and it's specification that he was able to figure out a solution to any problem which the customer faced.

Parth was now getting ready for the video shoot. He was wearing the blazer that he had gotten well ironed. He was also well shaved. He had taken the issue of shaving seriously again after Krisha and the showroom had come into his life. He just wanted to project himself well as a good prospect to her and as a professional customer service representative.

"With the launch of its first electric vehicle, the company is showing its commitment to the environment. This is Parth from the Concept Motor Showroom. This is the first car show of its kind and we are the biggest in the market. Come check us out, you will be wowed!"

Parth finished off his first video shoot as he ended with his name and credits to the showroom. The next shoot was going to be over a test drive.

Parth had never owned a car but he had his driving lessons and permanent license done as soon as he was eighteen. His father made sure of it. Though his dad never allowed them use his car, which was now out of vogue and hardly worked anyway.

By 5 PM, both videos had been shot and the videographer agreed to hand over the edited copies to Parth by the next evening.

*   *   *

"So when do you think I should meet your parents?" Parth asked Krisha.

"I don't want to put you under pressure Parth. Your family is easy going and liberal, mine is quite competitive and conservative. I only want you to come see my family when you are ready."

"I am ready to meet them now…or…is there something I am missing?"

"Parth you are like my life. I can't allow anyone distract you or mistreat you. I want you to concentrate on what you are doing here in Mumbai with the showroom. That place has caught a new vibe since you got there. Beside I really want us to get to know each other more and for me to settle in well into this new phase of my life. I have been heartbroken twice. I want to really grow into this."

"But you know I cherish you right? And I won't deliberately set out to hurt you or mistreat you like those scumbags. Come here honey, don't be scared. I see your point though, let's give it time."

"I love you Parth, I love you so so much…And though I hate to say it, but this is the truth, I don't know what I will do if I lose you. You are the best thing that ever happened to me. I have never met any man so real like you and I really want to get used to that before I present you to my family. My dad was relieved to see me home, and so was my step mom. But that old stale air of insatiable ambition filled the air, I bet this time the fight is more within the family than among allies and rivals outside the family".

"Wow…I had better keep my cool; I am just a small fry. Besides I have quite a humble background. I am still figuring out how my negligible salary will suffice."

"Parth, I believe in our future. I have some good savings and I know you will rise to the top. I mean you had the opportunity to pick a better paying position but you stuck with your passion. That's an investment and it will come back with returns. But whichever way I am fine with you."

"Krisha, I am just learning to take life one step at a time. I must be honest, it's like I am in a school. I believe as I pursue what's next, what should follow will naturally become clear. I am quite clear about a lot of things now, including money…as my personal value increases, I will ensure to invest my disposable income in other credible ventures. I picked a book recently."

"Parth you are amazing me…there is a sweetening sensation I feel everyday just thinking of us… trust me honey we deserve our time together before we face my family. There are things I still need to tell you because they are things you must know my love. And now that I think of it, I think the readiness issue is more on my side, I am not ready to face my family".

"You didn't say much of how reuniting with them went and I didn't want to push. Are you sure you are alright honey?"

"Dad was a bit ill when I arrived, but he was getting better by the time I was leaving. He looked old and I got scared. But other than that they are cool. My other brother is now married. He said he wasn't happy I wasn't there. I had to apologize. And then we played and laughed and also saw the politics my stepmother was playing for her boys. But we the kids are all cool, though they are still quite competitive."

"Let's see where we would be one year from now. What do you think?"

"Yes Parth, I feel your flow. That sounds more like it"

They played and chatted away the rest of the evening.

*   *   *

"So my computer skills aren't a waste after all." Parth was thinking out loud while he was editing and uploading the videos on the social video sharing sites. He was adding tags and keywords to the videos so that anyone who was searching the internet for that particular car and its reviews would find his video as the first one in the results. Parth had also added the logo of *The Concept Motors & Showroom* and con-tact details so that anyone who had instant query or wanted to make an instant booking could just call up the showroom.

"It's so amazing what Prabhudas said. When you love something, everything just starts working out for you. I hated to work on computers. But here I've managed to actually create a marketing video with me as a host."

It had now been days since Parth had uploaded the video on the internet. It was another regular but interesting day at the showroom for him. He was handling a few customers who had dropped in to check out the new electric car. After the question and answer sessions between him and the customers, Parth joined his colleagues over lunch.

"So what happened to the video shooting? I don't see any great change happening because of that yet." Manoj a senior colleague was asking Parth.

With the attention that Parth was getting, majority of his colleagues became fond of him, while there were some who had questions and doubts. Some others showed their skepticism out of jealousy. One day Parth had heard a discussion between two other staff from a different section.

"Don't you think he is a jerk? He sounds bad. He looks bad. Our showroom is going to suffer big time because of what he is doing."

"Only the rich buy these cars anyway and most of them don't use social media that much."

Parth overlooked the negativity. In one of the recent hang outs with Prabhudas, he had been warned that:

"When you create awareness, you are going to also face critics who are preoccupied with finding the neg-

ative side to everything. But you must stand tall and confident irrespective of whatever happens. The only thing that matters is the core. That is, the love that you have for what you do and the desire to make a difference. Everything else is simply noise. When you stand confident, the critics will also lose their patience one day and they will just give up."

Parth decided to explain things to this colleague of his and others who were standing-by and waiting for an answer.

"It's just been three days that I uploaded the videos. When I checked it this morning it already had about one thousand views. As the views grow, we will start seeing the results."

Most of his colleagues nodded, a few sneered. Parth suddenly felt like he was under pressure to deliver and perform. He couldn't understand why people he joined just a few weeks back expected so much from him. For the larger part he felt the love from most of them, but a few were obviously jealous. Whichever way, he felt the pressure. While some people looked up to him, a few others were waiting to see him fail.

*   *   *

As the week passed by Parth was elated and in fact surprised to see the views for the videos increase from a thousand views to about ten thousand by the end of the week. He expected it to climax at about three to four thousand.

By the following week, the effect of the videos began to have an impact on business in the showroom. A customer had called in recently asking about Parth. He had some doubt about one of the vehicles in the video and wanted Parth to clarify. There were also four customers who had never visited the showroom, but based on what they saw on the video made down payments for their cars. The security unit also recorded more influx of people by the middle of the week.

Parth was attending to a customer when he saw the owner of the showroom, Ashutosh, waiting at the head of the isle for him. He quickly rounded-up with the customer and directed her toward the booking department, as Ashutosh gradually approached him.

"The idea is working. We have seen 30-40% increase in the number of prospects walking into the showroom. And you should not be surprised to know that this time around that there are some of them in the lobby insisting they want to talk to you. They have seen you in that video and they are waiting for you to see them."

"Really? Wow…I am glad to help them in any way I can"

Parth had now been meeting more people than he used to.

"You have been handling them well. Don't you feel the pressure of the job now?"

"No pressure sir. Or at least I haven't noticed any yet."

"No Boy, you are handling more customers now than a week before. Usually in my experience, when there is a sudden flow of customers like this, most of the customer service representatives get easily stressed and try to avoid handling too many. Often in sales we have to then introduce incentives to keep our service representatives going. But in your case you are doing a very good job."

Parth was surprised. He did not even notice that he was actually handling more people than he was before. The new traffic was definitely as a result of the videos that were now being watched by many. It proved another of Prabhudas' wise sayings true:

"When you are in love, things start becoming effortless, you would not notice so much the occasional

ups and downs which most of the people without love find hard to tolerate".

He had found this to be true both at work and in his relationship. The love between Parth and Krisha had grown into a great burning light.

Parth was now even more motivated. He was thinking of new ideas that could create even more awareness for the showroom.

A couple of days after his conversation with Ashutosh, Parth was at his routine, highlighting different car features to a group of customers when he heard a loud call from Manoj."

"Parth. Can you please come over? There is someone on the phone asking for you."

"For me? Alright, I'll be there in a minute."

Parth wound up his discussion with the customers and asked a colleague to help him out with the rest while he moved towards the service desk to answer the phone.

"Hello, this is Parth, who am I speaking with?"

"Hi, this is Anita from the news channel *Headlines Today*. We are keen on doing a story with you on the new electric car out in the market. We were wondering if we can come over to your showroom and do the shooting."

Parth was surprised. While he was really excited about doing the story, he had a bit of a hesitation which he couldn't place his fingers on.

Parth then continued his dialogue with the lady on the phone.

"We are pleased by your offer, but kindly bear with me as I am not sure I can give you an answer right away. But please give me your mobile phone number so I can get back to you?"

"Sure. Please take it down."

As Parth put the phone down, he got a bit worried. He was starting to think that it was not simple anymore. He felt a prick from his old demons about not being good enough. He knew the moment he got to the limelight he would be more subject to criticism. Besides he wasn't the one doing the recording this time, this was a TV show hostess putting him in the spotlight. It was a big call and mistakes could be costly. He still doubted himself, especially now that things seemed so serious and going to the mainstream media.

He kept thinking to himself as he was closing for the day. Krisha had said she was going to drop by to drive him home, she just wanted to see him again, she couldn't wait till Sunday and wasn't satisfied with just chats.

"Learning about cars before getting this job was quite comfortable, only a few people knew about it. It was also fine when I got the job and uploaded those videos online; after all, only those looking for specific cars would know about me. But now if I do this, it will become a public face. Everyone will know about me. Everyone will start asking me questions and I don't if I am that good."

"Honey I have not met anyone better than you and I have met car dealers, trust me you are good."

"Coming from someone with your pedigree, what you just said makes me feel better. Thanks"

"And what if I add a kiss to it?" Krisha smiled.

"Then you will send me to the sweet bliss of *la la land* where all things are possible."

"I believe in you honey and I am here with you no matter what. Don't feel pressured. Do what you are comfortable with."

"Krisha, what would I do without you? You make me feel so complete"

As Parth's words sunk into the heart of Krisha, she couldn't believe her luck. He was the one who needed the encouragement and there he was validating her place in his life.

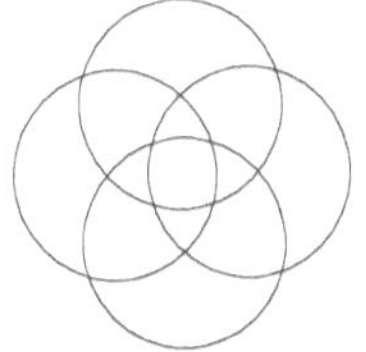

Chapter Eleven

The following day as Parth was closing from work, he knew he needed some clarity. He didn't feel scared anymore, but he needed to have an idea into how this move could help the showroom and his career. He needed to know what to expect after the TV show. It felt like he was moving to the next phase. Parth could no longer resist the urge; he was going to see Prabhudas.

"He will show me the way with his special insights. I want to see him."

As Parth walked outside the showroom. He was waiting for a cab which could take him to Prabhudas' office building. As he waved his hand to stop a cab, one came towards him and stopped in front of him.

"What!! Prabhudas? What a pleasant surprise, I was just going to your office to see you"

Parth was excited as he saw Prabhudas inside the cab. Prabhudas was just getting out of it.

"Well. I just thought I should see you and see how things are going."

"Like I said, I was just coming to see you. There is something which has made me sad and I have not been able to find an answer. I needed your help."

"Come here son, let's walk and talk."

"So…What's the problem."

"You know I created my video on the cars and uploaded it on the internet. This was to implement the element of success we last spoke about—the mass awareness. It is also working really well. The store is seeing rise in customers."

"But today, I got a call from a TV Channel which wants to do a recorded session with me on a particular car. The problem is it will become too public. How am I going to handle that? Besides, my friends and extended family will know about it. They still think I'm doing the other job which seemed more respectful. "

"And now, when they come to know about me working in the car showroom, I don't know how they will react. My parents worked so hard to provide quality education for us, I don't ever want them to be dishonoured."

"Son....What do you really want? What you love or everyone's opinion? The real question is, do you love what you are doing?"

"I'm absolutely enjoying it."

"Listen son, do you prefer the suicide jump? There is dignity in labour and you have a woman and your family supporting you, why do you want to compromise your life for the noise around you? Do what you really have a flare for and work hard at it, everyone who truly cares about you will eventually come around soon enough. Luckily for you, your parents are already on board. Nobody said it would be easy, but it's better than living your life to please others and suffering in silence."

"Hmmmmmnnn…you have a point Prabhu."

"You just sounded like Krisha. She is the one that calls me Prabhu."

Parth smiled.

"Parth, if you stand confident with what you love, those who oppose you will give up one day. If you stand for what you believe, they will lose their pointless arguments and that will be your real victory. Success only comes to those who care less about how people say their lives should be."

Parth was silent. There were many thoughts coming to his mind.

"This phase will lead you to a new level in your career. You will transition from just having a job to becoming a careerist as the company you work for will begin to value you differently."

"Thank you for showing me the way again Prabhu, now I am clear on what's next."

"Ok. So I got to get moving now. If anything else I am sure we would see." Prabhudas winked with a friendly mischief on his face as he made to take his leave.

Parth smiled and said "I know there is more to you Prabhu, one day I will figure it out"

He waved to Prabhudas who was now on his away.

*   *   *

The following morning at the office, Parth dialed the phone number of Anita from the News Channel.

"Hello Anita, Parth on the line. So when can we do this shooting?"

"My crew will can come over by 2pm today if you are fine with it. They will need an hour to do the setup. I will be there by 3pm and then we'll start."

"OK sure."

Parth remembered he hadn't carried Ashutosh along, though parth knew he wouldn't have an objection since he had given him the go ahead from the beginning. He dialed his number

"Hello sir, there is a news channel that wants to do a TV recording for the new electric car. They are coming in by 2pm, I was wondering if we could have the pleasure of your presence on set sir."

"Oh Great! But I have to go for a meeting. I'm sure you will be able to handle everything Parth. I will tell Manoj to give whatever assistance is required for the shooting."

Parth headed for home late that day. By the time he left the complex, it was 8:00 PM. He had called Krisha after the session to tell her about it. After the official closing hours, he spoke to her for another thirty minutes. He wished they were married, but he knew things were only just taking shape.

He had not informed his parents earlier about the recording. He knew that the video shoot done that day was going to be telecast on the news channel for the next 24 hours, in some cases it lasted longer. The main interview will be twenty-five minutes, but the hostess will engage the audience for five minutes first, and then in between there will be commercials for ten minutes.

They had finished at about 3:40pm, and the hostess had wanted to have a brief chat with him. She liked his passion and wondered if there were other things they could do regarding cars, she wanted him to call if he had any ideas. She said her producer wanted it to feature on their program later that night.

As Parth walked down the street, he thought of it that the program may have aired on the TV already and he was wondering if anyone had seen it. He really didn't care what his colleagues or people like Ashwini would think; after all, he was enjoying every second of his job and was now starting to become famous.

He arrived home.

"Come Parth. We're so happy. We got some phone calls saying you were on TV. They were asking us about it. It featured briefly in the news and they say it will come up fully after the news." Parth's mother said as he entered the house.

"Yes. Right mum."

"Get fresh and we'll have dinner. I hear there will be a replay again sometime tomorrow. We are proud of you son".

Parth heaved a sigh of relief and settled down. He was the happiest man on earth.

"And we have with us here today, Parth from the Conept car showroom who will answer our questions about the new electric car."

The camera then moved over to Parth as he started talking. Parth's parents fixed their gaze on the TV. No one else from the family had ever featured on television. Parth's younger brother Tejas was also happy as he saw his brother on TV.

This was the second time Parth had himself on a video but the very first time on TV. His eyes became misty as he kept watching.

There were commercials in between, and after about 45 minutes the program was over. What Parth's parents had seen created a good impression on their minds. Now they were just silent. Parth's mother reflected on their last conversation about the showroom job and the loan company.

Abhay wondered where he got all that knowledge from. "Was he studying automobiles while we thought he was learning computer technology?" He thought to himself.

They had good family time talking about careers and life. Tejas, who had recently returned from school and had been posted to an organization in Mumbai for his internship, found an opportunity to share about his career path and decisions with the family. Abhay and Subhada felt proud that their children had turned out with fine ideals. They were not rich as a family, but they were fulfilled, and surely they were not as poor as where they had come from. Life was indeed getting better.

*   *   *

The following morning at about 9:20am when they were rounding up with breakfast and starting to have their normal chit-chat, the door bell rang. It was a Sunday and everyone was in a relaxed mood. Abhay didn't like the disturbance and went to check who was at the door himself. He was determined to dismiss the person soon enough.

As Abhay looked through the peephole, he saw the gentle woman from the next flat and his disturbed face formed quickly into a grin. He whispered to his family "It is sweet Mrs. Amble". He was grinning from ear to ear.

"I am the only one who is sweet Abhay", Subhada said with mischief in her voice. They all suddenly laughed and forgot Mrs. Aadhira Amble was at the door."

Abhay opened the door and greeted Mrs. Amble, "You are most welcome. Come join us, we are having a wonderful family time."

"Thank you Mr. Bhandari, please is Parth home?" asked the lady who had her teenage son with her.

"Yes. He is here. Please come in."

"We saw Parth on TV last night and wanted to get some guidance from him for the future of my son who wants to become an automobile engineer."

Parth's parents were astonished. Parth was surprised too. What had been a struggle between guilt and disappointment some weeks ago was now turning into a thing of pride. The popularity had started.

"Please have your sit, you are most welcome. We just finished breakfast, and Parth will be happy to join you." Parth's mother said with a proud voice.

"You are a big man now Parth, you are on TV and all. Can you please guide my son who wants to become an automobile engineer on what he should do next? He has just finished his 10th."

Parth was happy to give the lady's son some tips on cars and the automobile field as a whole. He advised the boy to read some books and also read books such as "The Toyota Way."

After the lady moved out, Parth was sitting on his chair when his father came towards him and touched his shoulder.

"Son, you have made us proud. No one has ever consulted me for what they wanted to do in the future. And here you are, so young, yet you are on TV. You have had the guts to stand for what you love. I'm a proud father." His father's eyes were wet.

Parth's mother came towards him and she started crying too.

"I promise you one thing mom and dad, I'll always honour your investments in this family and the ideals you instilled in us, and may god give us the fulfillment of a better and prosperous life."

In the days and weeks ahead, more and more channels were to come to the Concept car showroom to conduct TV shows with Parth on various cars. Parth was now totally free of tensions and pressure because his initiative had proven a success. He was also happy about the fact that he was stable. He had gained stability and confidence, and his work was now being noticed both at work, among his peers, among his neighbours and with his family. For him, the popularity didn't matter as much as the dignity it conferred on his work.

Parth was now to be seen frequently on TV automobile shows. He got both appreciation and criticism about his analyses and kept getting even better at it.

Although Parth's celebrity status was growing, his was still earning the 8,000 rupees a month at the showroom. In one corner of his mind, he was increasingly getting concerned about when that will change.

*   *   *

Krisha woke that Sunday morning a bit late and was feeling a bit numb. She had been working so hard for the past couple of weeks. She had asked Parth to come by during lunch the previous afternoon to see the space she had gotten for the gallery. Parth had been so excited about it all, that she felt a bit awkward. Most of the men she had known in her life had been her competitors even when they were in a relationship with her. This felt different. They snacked while they looked around, and when it was time for him to go, he brought out an old bottle of wine from his back pack and gave it to her.

"Wow, this is so nice. How did you get this? I know it's really expensive."

"Ashutosh gave it to me as a gift with a little note, he said something like *'This is for you Parth, your passion, commitment and value is rare.'* I felt a bit flattered. In that moment, I looked at myself and I knew he didn't know me. All I could think of was you. It just dawned on me in a funny way that you had committed yourself to me and loved me so unconditionally even when you saw how ruffled I was. Suddenly realized you knew all along that I was troubled. I didn't look good at that café that day, I know I didn't".

"Parth, I have never met any man more real than you in my life. I would have said same about

Prabhudas, but there is more to him it seems. He seems quite superhuman or something, I can't place it. But for you, my life hasn't been the same since I met you. I feel more human than I have ever felt."

Abhay had just fixed his old car recently. He was planning a trip to the site during the week. Parth pleaded to use the car on Sunday, which was the next day, and his dad agreed.

After Parth left Krisha that afternoon for the showroom, Krisha couldn't hold it anymore. She cried her eyes out and closed for the day. When she got back home, she brought out all her art pieces and set them up. Something kept telling her she was more worthy than she ever thought—it was Parth's voice, she kept hearing it.

She dialed his number as she rolled to the other side of the bed.

"Parth, I feel so tired today, I don't think I can do any outing, could we meet at my place? I have something for you."

Two hours later, Parth was at the door. Krisha was a bit apprehensive; she wasn't sure what his response would be.

"Hi Parth, wow nice car, please come in."

Parth winked and he made his way in.

"Un…be…lieve…able…"

Parth couldn't believe his eyes. He looked at every piece in awe and tears formed in his eyes as he saw the pain and fear embedded in some of the works and the pure beauty of imagination in others.

"You mean you have been hiding all of these for years? Why? I am not so good at graphics, but when I see an art work of class I can tell. There are no words to really describe these paintings Krish, they are indescribable and out of this world."

Krisha told him about each work, what inspired her and what they meant. She talked some more about her past, her struggles, her decisions and her victories.

They talked about many things and about their expectations for marriage. Parth raised his concerns about finances—he didn't want them to struggle.

They spent a good amount of time in each other's company before Parth returned home that evening.

*   *   *

Parth got up very early the following morning with one question on his mind—"what is next?"

Parth realized one truth about life that day, when one challenge ends, another one begins.

"I think I should go to the office building and see Prabhudas." Parth remembered the discussion about five elements of success and he knew there was more to come up.

He wanted to get there before 7am so he could have enough time with Prabhudas. He asked his father for his car and drove off at 6:20am.

Parth approached the security guards again. While he was about to ask one of the security guards, he could hear a familiar voice from behind.

"Welcome my son. I was expecting you."

"Oh, really?"

"Didn't I tell you? Whenever you need my help, I will always be there."

"Yes, I remember that." Parth replied, a bit troubled about the sense of mysticism that flashed through his mind about Prabhudas' increasingly mysterious ways.

"So, should we take a walk?"

Parth and Prabhudas started walking through the business district.

"You know, I was wondering. It's been about three months now. I really feel my life is changed. I am enjoying every day as it comes. People are starting to know me now, but I am thinking about my financial future."

"Yes. Today we will come to that. But you see Parth, the whole professional life of a man is like a car; the heart is the engine and everything else moves when the engine starts working."

Parth was listening carefully. Parth got more curious as he listened to the analogies given by Prabhudas.

"So you've started your engine. You've found what you love. You know the four angles to it. You have also become recognized for your proficiency through some form of awareness. Now it's about putting it into gear and moving ahead. I'm about to tell you about two other important elements of success. Now it is about how you can earn money from what you love and how you can grow your financial strength."

"Yes. In fact that's why I am here. I was just about to ask you about it."

"Good then. We are on track. Let's drive towards the showroom so you are not late for work. We can talk in the car. I had just signed out from my shift when you came in, so we can continue during your lunch."

"Wow, you would do that for me? Thank you so much. But you should be tired."

"I am fine son, trust me."

"You know Prabhudas…There is one thing that has become clear to me. I used to think that when you become famous, you earn money, but surely it doesn't work that way."

"Becoming famous has to do with what you can do, you ability to excel in it and people getting to know you for your work. But being rich is about how good your financial understanding is."

"Financial understanding...I see."

"Tell me Parth. How do you know when someone is successful?"

"When he has a lot of money."

"Money to do what?"

"To get his basic necessities. To buy what wants."

"Right, there you are. So what are these basic necessities?"

"A good house, a car, and a good bank statement that takes care of the family and basic luxuries such as trips, good college education and other good things of life."

"Lets talk about some successful people now. For an example, let's talk about your favourite cricketer. Sachin Tendulkar."

"By now you know that he is famous because he loves to play cricket and he plays it well."

"Yea."

"And you know he is rich."

"Yes."

"But tell me son. When you say he is rich. Do you mean to say that he carries a truckload of cash with him?"

"No. He is rich because he has a big house. He drives super luxury cars and he travels the world and lives a happy life."

"Precisely. But do you think they are still his basic needs?"

Parth was thinking. He was imagining the life of successful people had he seen.

"In a way, yes. He is so busy but he gets extra comfort with his house, his car and other things."

"Son. To begin with the next two elements, you are going to have to understand how money was started in first place."

Prabhudas took out a Rs. 2000 note to Parth and asked him.

"Do you think this existed since man was born?"

"I don't think so."

"What do you think about this note?"

"This is what everyone needs. These days, one is expected to get more and more of this."

"There is the flaw son. This is how most people misunderstand everything and that is where the problem starts. You see son, this is just the paper. Those who chase this, get nothing in the end, because this is temporary. It's going to vanish soon with the demands of life. Whoever wants to chase this is going to have a similar experience."

"What do you mean?"

"To understand this, we will have to take your mind back in time; a time when there was no paper like this."

Parth had his eyes wide open as he was listening to Prabhudas.

"We just talked about basic needs, didn't we?"

"Yes."

"You know back in time people used to exchange the basic necessities directly."

"True"

"Those who had cows that gave milk exchanged them for those who had chicken that laid out eggs in a proportion they agreed were equivalent. Those who had grains exchanged it for those who produced the cut wood that could be built into a house."

Parth was listening very carefully."

"Everyone exchanged whatever basic need they had in surplus for what they needed, but which others had in surplus. People even exchanged farmlands which produced grains when they needed medical treatment to be alive."

"Rich people were called rich people because they had more of the basic needs of what other people would need."

"But then how did money come in?"

"There was a problem with establishing certain trades. When a person was to trade within his community, within his village, it was fine. He could manage the exchange of basic needs."

"But as people started traveling and were looking to trade with other people from far villages on other strategic articles of trade, carrying the basic necessities started to become painful and cumbersome. Imagine that you had to carry a truckload of cows or chicken which you had to trade against a truckload of wood."

"Right. That must have been painful."

"It was not just painful, but there was a risk of dacoits looting everything a man had as the man was carrying the goods with him. It was easier to rob him."

"So some smart People found a solution to that problem by introducing money."

"So a man could instead just exchange money for what he wanted to trade. So an "x" number of currency notes equaled to a certain number of cows, and a "Y" number of currency notes equaled a certain number of chickens and wood and so on."

"Soon, societies began to find it so easier to make trades with paper, so they he started to use currency instead of things like precious metals, jewellery and swords, for their needs such as wood, chicken, cows, etc."

"Wow. So that's how humans started using the notes. But then why is it that people do bad things for this paper."

"That's the glory of human life. The problems will never end. With the currency notes, human solved one problem but other ones emerged."

Parth's resumption time had come. They had been in the parking lot for a while. They stepped out and agreed to meet during lunch. Prabhudas will wait at the cafeteria.

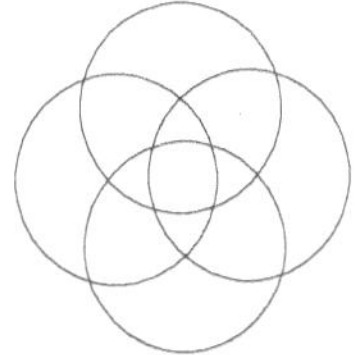

Chapter Twelve

During lunch, Parth located Prabhudas in the cafeteria and they continued.

"So Prabhudas you said new problems emerged."

"Yes. Soon, people started thinking that this paper was the secret to achieving happiness and the secret to get everything that they needed; so then all sorts of crimes started. Whoever had more of this paper was called rich and people started believing in doing whatever to get more of this little paper which simply started as a medium to trade the basic necessities of life."

Parth followed the thoughts closely.

"All that mattered for humans was to choose whatever gave them more of paper. The basic necessities were forgotten. So the basic foundation of money and financial intelligence is to be able to provide necessities to other people and to meet necessities of your own. If you can play any role in meeting other people's needs or interests, you will be able to meet your own as well. And this is how you can be successful financially."

Parth was silent while Prabhudas was talking. He kept wondering how this would translate to better earnings for him.

"I already earn Prabhudas, but I don't earn enough, yet I believe I am bringing real value to the company."

"You see Parth. When you joined this organization, what you started with was the estimated value of someone at that level of entry point on the job. As the company begins to see you are of a higher value, they will make you a better offer except they are willing to lose you."

"I see…so you think Ashutosh will give me a raise soon?"

"If he hasn't yet, it must be for a reason. People are in business to make profit; therefore, they must assess the degree of profitability you are bringing in, the sustainability of any package they are to give to you, and then your loyalty."

"How then do successful professionals earn fat salaries?"

"It all boils down to their estimated value as professionals and the estimated value of a job title. Don't forget you were offered another job that had a higher estimation in value. Tell me, what do you think would happen if you were to apply to another organization now with your current popularity?"

"I...I would get a better offer. Are you kidding me? I never thought of it that way."

"You see Ashutosh gave you a platform, without that nobody would have known you. But you have also in return justified that confidence and brought him more customers. So he is already coming under pressure not to lose you, yet he can't stop you from doing what you are doing because he needs the customers to keep coming. But for you it is important to know you haven't arrived yet, you need to really consolidate on your strengths."

"I see."

"But a salary isn't what is going to get you that rich. Let's go over this together, mention any successful celebrity you know."

"Well. Let's say Amitabh Bacchan."

"Okay. So how did you get to know him?"

"I see him in the movies. He is a great actor."

"Yes. Being a good actor makes him known to millions of people and he becomes famous by doing that."

"Where else do you see him feature?"

"Where else? Well on billboards, and in adverts generally."

"Exactly. Now what are these products that he poses for?"

"It's something that people buy."

"Exactly. The houses, clothes, soaps, electronics, etc. which people need. And he is paid for these adverts because his fame has become tradable. They also do other things using their fame as leverage."

"So what you are saying is he is rich because of his estimated worth and also because he helps other businesses outside his immediate industry sell their products?"

"Exactly."

Parth's eyes widened with realization. "So you mean the opportunities keep coming towards famous people and they get a chance to choose opportunities to earn more money, whether it's a new job, endorsement deals or other projects?"

"Now you get it. And that's in the case of celebrities and fame. For some others it is professional pedigree and the credibility of their name, work and ideas. In order cases such as in a new business, it is the risks and inputs the investors or entrepreneurs bring in that matters when the venture succeeds."

Parth was still silent. Never before had he heard such a simple and straightforward explanation on how successful people made money.

He was thinking to himself "The successful people carry so much aura that one often overlooks how they actually become rich."

They ate their lunch.

"It's so delicious." Parth said as he tasted the soup.

"Yes. Their restaurants are well known for good local dishes."

"You mean Ashutosh owns other restaurants?"

"Yes his family does, just like your actor who owns that café we usually go to."

"Oh really? Despite being so successful, you mean he is a business man? Well he has the money anyway so he could have afforded to pay for it without blinking."

"Well it will actually be expensive to buy now, but he bought it when it was still an upcoming area which had the advantage of being a road touch property. And he bought it eight years back at nearly one tenth the current price."

"Remember one thing son: success is never permanent just as failure is never final. He bought it to retain his success and grow it."

"So successful people keep growing their wealth. That's interesting. "

"One needs to retain his success and grow it so that it can remain. Do you know what this place where your showroom now stands used to look like?"

"There was really nothing here I presume?"

"Absolutely nothing. You know what Ashutosh and his family do?"

"Yes, I am told they are in the real estate business and have great buildings."

"Well, there is a slight correction there. They don't just have great buildings; in their own case, they often build them. They also convert dilapidated or open spaces like this into magnificent pieces or businesses."

"Oh, I understand. So they grow their success as well? Like the famous actor. They convert something which is lesser in value into something that is higher in value."

"Not just that. They also sell a basic need, right?"

"Yes I see that people need property, and they also need cars. So people keep patronizing them and the cash keeps coming in."

"Didn't I tell you that you are smart? You are such a beautiful person on the inside, and you learn very fast."

Parth was smiling. He could not believe how Prabhudas had converted his disappointments and depression in life into an experience he now loved to live.

"But tell me Prabhudas, how do I use all this to my benefit?"

"Son, taking the first step and a series of other baby steps is what you have done up till now, and those keys form the foundation for a successful life. All I have done is to tell you the basics, but you are going to have to build the rest from here on by yourself. Ponder on these two elements I just shared, gradually build your success and keep growing it."

"It's time to get back to work son. I should also head back, got some more places to visit." Prabhudas had a knowing smile on his face.

"Thanks so much Prabhu…life looks better from where I stand now."

"You know son, you really wanted your life turned around, now you have it and you will keep having new chapters as you journey on. But always remember, when you really need my help, I am always around."

"Great. So when next will I see you?"

"Will you?"

"Of course I will Prabhu, or are you going somewhere?"

"I am confident now that you can handle things on your own son."

"Parth! Come over you got one of those stubborn clients who wants just you!"

"Alright, I will be there in a minute."

"You know what Prabhudas, I will come over to your house or office when I want to see you, just that your phone isn't reachable these days. Please keep it on".

"Sure Parth, my line will always be on when you need to reach me" Prabhudas said with a smile as he stood there waving at Parth.

*   *   *

It was now six months since Parth resumed at the showroom. In the last two months he had held several interviews on TV, radio, magazines, newspapers and on popular blogs and vlogs. Media outfits from neighbouring cities and towns were also joining in scheduling shows. A new trend was beginning in the industry and the showroom was experiencing quantum levels of sales that transcended the immediate precincts of Mumbai. The digital team had upgraded the online platform to attend to the demands of customers from across the country while sales kept climbing.

These days it was getting more and more difficult to arrange the shooting of reviews at the showroom. The reason was that more customers were starting to choose *The Concept Motors Showroom* over others. The social video publicity and news channel reviews had worked so well that the showroom had witnessed a triple digit growth in its traffic and so the demand on personnel was intense.

It was clear that the business was achieving its sales numbers faster than expectations even when there were no sales mandates given to employees to meet. Parth had come in from nowhere and had almost single handedly deployed his passion towards the growth of the business.

Ashutosh had called for a workers' retreat that Sunday and booked an exclusive treat for them at the Golden Gate Resort. Ashutosh began by saying,

"I want to express my profound gratitude to every single member of the team for the great work you all have contributed to the success of our showroom. I am declaring a special bonus package for every member of staff".

"Woooh!!!!!!!!!!!!" the room resounded with shouts of excitement and rounds of applause.

"We have exceeded our initial projections for the entire year in just six months and the business landscape has changed on account of our activities. Our competitors are regrouping, which has necessitated that we also re-organize our activities".

Ashutosh christened the team #TheGoldenTeam and gave every member of staff a special plaque. All customer service representatives were elevated to sales supervisors. Special awards were also given to outstanding members of the team that had put in more time and had handled more customers. The star award was given to Parth for his invaluable contribution to the organization. The entire room roared in excitement and applause as Parth walked up to collect his award.

"I must say that we admire you for your innovative ideas, humility and unmatched dedication to duty. Many of your colleagues do not know that you have a college degree and actually turned down an attractive offer in the ICT department, but today you have made an indelible impact here with us."

As Ashutosh made these remarks many of the ladies screamed. Parth was elevated to the newly created position of Customer Relations Manager (CRM) and he was to report directly to Ashutosh. The former Manager of the showroom was now the Business Development Manager (BDM), who would maintain business relations with the car manufacturers, supervise logistics for any new outlets or aspects of the business that would be opened, and oversee sales and accounts throughout the organization.

Manoj was elevated to Executive Assistant and Principal Secretary to Ashutosh.

Ashutosh continued, "The Human Resource Manager has requested that we do intensive trainings over the remaining part of the year to adapt our activities in the last six months into a sales strategy for every staff to imbibe, so that the Sales Supervisors can implement them when they are posted to the new outlets across India in six months from now.

Two supervisors will be posted to each outlet; one would oversee customer relations and report to the CRM, while the other will oversee sales and accounts and report to the BDM. The Information and Communications Manager is working on a powerful digital network that will connect us all. Cheers and have fun everyone!"

Ashutosh had a meeting with the new management team and asked them to work together to advance new ideas and projects that could move the organization forward.

*   *   *

Krisha had a tough time getting business development, branding and marketing experts to develop a workable curriculum for artistes. She wanted something simple that wouldn't alter the originality of these artistes.

"Parth, Art is delicate. It often reflects those shades of human qualities that fight not to be suppressed; such as *tranquility, simplicity, the beauty of the soul, activism, difference, expression, reflection, solitude, truth, nature and its beauties, pain, weakness, hubris, and the infinite human potential.* The course modules prepared by these experts will speak above the heads of these folks. I understand them, but can't they simplify it? It's just tiring. Gosh!"

"Hey honey", Parth touched her arms gently and wrapped his arms around her,

"If there is anyone who can simplify those things, it is you honey. You are like a bridge. You have seen it all. From the discouragement of a father in pursuing your artistic talent, to working in competitive environments, to closing topnotch business deals, building new markets and handling corporate image branding, you have it all honey. You understand the language of both worlds. Remember what Prabhudas said."

"I just wish he was here", Krisha said.

Since the day Prabhudas said bye to Parth at the showroom, they had not seen him. Parth and Krisha had been to the tower several times. All the security guards working at the building had told Parth that they had not known anyone by the name of Prabhudas and that they had not seen a man in the descriptions they had given. They had even been to the temple complex where Prabhudas claimed to be staying. However even there, they didn't find anything until someone pointed them to the leader who said they may have actually met with a divine being.

"So was he lying all those times he said he had shifts?"

"No, that he said he had a shift didn't have to be a lie. God doesn't work alone, and he definitely didn't come for you both alone, he must have had other people in mind. Don't also forget he never stopped overseeing world affairs for a minute. And truly he and Mother Nature are loving partners. They work hand-in-hand. God is in love with nature and humanity"

Krisha had tried to make sense of it all.

"I have never really been religious, so why would any divine being take such an interest in me?" she queried.

But she had remembered that night she prayed before leaving home, and also when she prayed about Parth—perhaps all that had happened in the last three years of her life had been answers to her prayers, she wondered.

Parth kept asking himself "Who was he? Was he really god? Was it that my faith had bought him to me? Or was he just a figment of my imagination that appeared at the right time when I was vulnerable?"

He really felt overwhelmed by the possibility of it all being some divine intrusion to help him.

"But Krisha saw him too, at least that means I am still sane."

"But it's been like magic. All the disappointments, pain, and negativity I had carried around no longer burden me and I am on the path of success", Parth thought to himself.

Parth remembered some words from Prabhudas that day.

"Son, taking the first step and a series of other baby steps is what you have done up till now... but you are going to have to build the rest from here on by yourself...I am confident now that you can handle things on your own..."

* * *

Parth knew he hadn't arrived yet, but he had paid his dues. He knew it was time for him to maximize his opportunities.

He suggested that the showroom create two magazines every quarter to capture happenings in the automobile industry, including the auto sports world. One publication should specially be created for staff to help the knowledge of those in sales while the other should be for the entire industry with the label of the showroom as the prominent brand image.

Parth also met with Ashutosh to discuss the possibility of having some flexibility with his work and time. He would give full attention to his managerial roles, but would want to be able to honour other invitations that would give him necessary exposure. He offered to use those platforms where possible as an opportunity to market *"The Concept Motors & Showrooms"* as an organization, and wouldn't sign any contract with any other car dealer or showroom company. He wanted to be able to do endorsements.

"Are you sure the manufacturing companies will not feel that your endorsement with one of their competitors will unduly bias our minds and customers against the sales of their products?"

"My endorsement deals for now will not be with car manufacturers, it will focus on car products such as engine oils, car security systems, batteries, etc, and events such as TV shows, events sponsors etc. But like I said, everywhere I go people will know I am from *"The Concept Motors"* and we could also use that as a launch pad for our new showrooms in order to help our expansion drive. We should also hype our motor sports brands some more and make strategic alliances there. There is a lot more to discuss as the days unfold."

"I accept your offer Parth, I believe we can work together as partners and sign a contract that would protect our mutual interests."

* * *

One day, Parth had just finished the shooting of a newly upgraded car product that had just been launched. Aditi, the TV Presenter was still packing her setup with her team when her phone rang. It was her Editor-in-Chief, Raman.

"Hi Aditi, I was just taking a look at the video clippings by Parth, this guy is amazing. The responses to the videos have been huge and the feedback very good too. I was wondering if you could invite him over."

"Well sir, I am actually still with him at the Showroom. We were covering a feature on the new car just launched."

"Oh great. Why don't you ask him to come with you if he doesn't mind, I will be at the office."

Parth signaled to his assistant that he was leaving early. It was just 4pm. He still had Krisha's Gala night later that evening. She had succeeded in bringing together top artistes, leading figures and organizations in the arts collections industry, captains of industries, leading policy makers, and experts from across different fields such as the academia, the business world, the media, social influencers, and leaders from other corporate entities. They were already lodged in different hotels in Mumbai and had come from different countries across the world.

Krisha had remembered Prabhudas' advice not to abandon her established market and that was what she was doing. She wanted these established names to grace the new gallery with their name and give it the necessary prestige as a good lead off. Her efforts with the local market was also yielding fruit as she had made strategic alliances with policy makers, leaders in the public and private sectors across different fields. For now she was working on market and socio-cultural analysis curriculum for artistes.

Krisha felt new life flowing through her. There was an undeniable sense of fulfillment and deep level of inspiration that thrilled her entire being. She was making a difference and had found her mission, what she was doing now was to be a bridge between two worlds, create a new kind of awareness that will further lift the prestige and credence of the arts, and help develop the potentials of new artistes for the local market. It was truly a breath of fresh air for her.

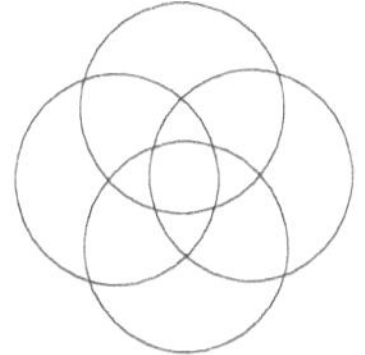

Chapter Thirteen

Parth was walking towards Raman's cabin. He was excited when Aditi told him about Raman, her boss, who had requested to see him at the office. Parth knew that Raman managed a prominent group of media companies consisting of news channels, newspapers and magazines.

"Come in Parth. I'm glad you are here."

"My pleasure sir."

"Well, I have seen the car comparison series conducted by you at your showroom; it's really been well received. You have also become a celebrity. I have received about twenty odd calls with people on the other line asking of you."

"Wow, is it? Thanks for the compliment, I just love to do what I do and make a difference."

"And it's really working well. So I thought it would be good we got to know each other you know."

"It's really a pleasure meeting you sir. Your contributions in the media are well known and I really respect the leadership you have provided for the various teams you lead. It will be great to see opportunities where we could work together now or in the future."

"You know Parth, the next few months are power-packed. There are major auto shows in four different cities in the world. There will be the bigwigs from the auto industry visiting there and we are short of people who can cover the event."

"Okay." Parth said, nodding thoughtfully. He remembered Prabhudas had said social events meet people's social needs.

A human being is a social person. Social gatherings are everyone's need and a lot of successful people earn money by playing a part in them.

"Well, so you know I was meeting some people who can possibly cover the event for us. It will only be a limited time assignment and we will be providing travel food stay and 75,000 rupees for every event which will last for about 4-5 days."

Parth tried to hide his amazement and surprise as he listened to Raman.

Raman continued. "Well Parth, I was thinking if you could be available for this short assignment? But let me tell you once again, this is not a job offer. I just wanted someone capable to handle the event for us."

Parth out of sheer foresight had made his move with Ashutosh before this new offer. He remembered all that Prabhudas had said about new offers, value, endorsements and all.

In split seconds Parth started thinking, "…75,000 rupees and international trips for a cumulative of five days? So that's like many times my salary and a chance to see the world."

Parth was still silent. He was thinking of how best to react to this.

"Yes, I would love to do it. I will just want to request that we present this coverage like a sort of collaboration between you and *The Concept Motors & Showroom.* Of course you will be the bigger partner."

"I must say I am a business man Parth, it would be nice to see your organization play on this kind of stage, but it should be willing to pay its way there. So it should foot at least twenty percent of the bill and we would gladly accept but only for those 4-5 days depending on what's workable for you. Let me know if we have a deal."

"I believe we do."

"You sure you don't want to talk it over with your folks?"

"We have an arrangement already."

"Great, I love that. I look forward to a great time then Parth, thanks for coming around."

Parth was willing to part with twenty percent of the deal to honour his agreement with Ashutosh. As far as he was concerned, it was still a fair deal.

Now Parth saw how useful those days of buying car magazines in college and following up on them so passionately, were now redefining his life.

As the elevator opened on the ground floor he muttered to himself, "Truly success is equal to preparedness + opportunity."

He couldn't wait to share the news with Krisha as he drove towards her office.

*   *   *

"Hi honey you are here, I am so happy to see you."

Krisha ran towards him and jumped into his arms, he looked so charming and so sturdy. She could see he had brought along his change of clothes for the night.

"I am right here by you honey, all the way. I am going nowhere else."

"it's been so tasking honey, I feel like I might stutter on that stage."

"Naaaah, not you honey, you are too polished to be caught unawares."

"Well coming from a screen god, I would say thanks for the flatter. I will feel more comfortable looking into your eyes all through the event though. So your seat will be strategic; and please honey keep looking into my eyes."

"You got me honey, you got me. I am all yours, do as you please."

Krisha had a line-up of classic presentations and a special feature on three of some of the most sought after pieces and the unique messages embedded in their thrust.

Someone shouted from the crowd "Tell me these art pieces will be on the stand tomorrow pleeeaassee! I will outbid anyone for at least one of them."

Krisha had brought up those presentations to create suspense in the hearts of the guests. Those who knew their onions well didn't bother their minds. They knew which collectors had the items and that they were not selling at the moment. But they were sure this event could raise the value of those items, and Krisha was sure to get a percentage from the eventual sale, if the market value increased by virtue of her event.

After the speeches and special appearances were announced, and the presentations concluded, the dance floor was opened and drinks and special snacks flowed freely.

As Parth and Krisha danced, they chatted quietly.

"It was a huge success my lady. How did you know all these people?"

"I was scared Parth. Even when many of them said they were in town, I still didn't believe they would come until I saw them here, it simply unbelievable."

"But I always believed you will do an excellent job. Only that this is really beyond excellence; it is pure genius. You have a beautiful mind and heart honey. I am in awe of you and I will always be come rain or shine."

"Krisha felt the thrills of his words sweeten her being as she felt lighter. She felt on top of the world."

"Honey, let us go meet our guests" Krisha requested.

They joined the different clusters of chat groups and exchanged pleasantries and introductions.

Later on, Krisha called for a toast and announced that the gallery would be open for 9am the following day.

Parth drove her home that night in his new official car. She had preferred taking taxis because she didn't want to drive. As he drove down to her place, he shared the news of the five day auto sports tour and the offer that had been made to him. She screamed in excitement. He dropped her off with a kiss and headed home.

*   *   *

When Parth had first told his parents about his promotion to the position of Customer Relations Manager, Subhada had screamed loudly. He had never seen her express herself in such a wild manner. She looked at him in astonishment as though he was a god.

His dad had jumped up from the couch and danced round the living room. He bowed severally as a form of worship to god and said,

"So I was not a fool after all. Life is so funny. From computer engineering to Customer Relations Manager…life is full of surprises."

"Parth, you dad and I were getting worried. You had become so popular, but we couldn't yet see any financial benefits. We had expected the company to promote you immediately and at a point we felt it might never happen. We were really bothered for you. We saw how hard you worked."

"Yes, I must say I was a bit worried to, but after speaking to Prabhudas, who surprisingly seems to have disappeared from the surface of the earth, I was really consoled. He taught me quite a lot that I have put into practice and I am now benefitting from."

They spent so much time that night talking about life, the ironies, contradictions and surprises.

It became clear to them later that he had truly reached his take-off to new heights when he brokered the new deal with Raman.

*　*　*

During the week, Parth subsequently discussed the deal with Ashutosh and they worked out necessary arrangements to cover for the days of his absence. Ashutosh also offered 35,000 rupees to cover part of the money Parth had forfeited from the original deal. And arrangements were made.

*　*　*

Parth was in Frankfurt for one of the motor shows. It was the second city in the lineup as they looked at strategies employed by the electric car manufacturers and other environmentally friendly efforts by other car manufacturers. Parth was just getting out of the suite arranged for him at the Hilton Hotel.

The Hilton hotel was only a couple of blocks from the Congress Center.

The exhibitions would have over two hundred different cars in all by the world's leading car manufacturers. At the exhibitions were head honchos of car manufacturers, government dignitaries and corporate officials from some of the most powerful countries and organizations around the world.

Parth entered the venue with his crew in excitement as he gave instructions. It was a tedious task to cover all the cars that would be on display for the entire five days, and covering all the events in the designated cities days. Though the days had been spaced, it involved really tedious activities; but Parth was hardly disturbed by the amount of work to be done. His excitement about the events overshadowed the jet lag and exertion that came with each outing.

The first event took place in Beijing, and Krisha had insisted on coming with him. She wanted to be part of the fun, socially since the first event was in Asia. Besides she couldn't imagine being away from him for two whole weeks. They could at least be together when he was off duty, and then go to the airport to embark on their different flights when it was time to go to Frankfurt—she would simply return to Mumbai.

She had said she would also join him for the last event in Dubai, where she was scheduled to attend a major exhibition and fair a day before.

As Parth was nearing the stall for BMZ motors, a well dressed official in suit approached him.

"Are you Parth?"

"Yes?" Parth was a bit surprised as he did not know who the person was.

"I am Julian Benske, I am the personal assistant to Mr. Schraff, the MD and Chairman of BMZ cars."

"Oh. Nice to meet you sir."

"Mr. Schraff was wondering if you could join us for dinner tonight. This is the last event our Chairman will be taking part in and he has expressed his intention to meet with some of the best presenters around the world."

"Oh is it? I am glad for the invitation, I will be there."

Julian gave him an invitation card that contained the time and venue.

*   *   *

Later that evening at the event, Parth was greeted by the Chairman and MD of BMZ cars.

"Hi Parth. How are you doing?"

"I'm fine sir and thanks for inviting me. It's been a wonderful experience. Cars have always been things I really love, and it's a privilege to meet the head of a company that actually makes one of the finest brands."

Schraff smiled.

"So how did you start your career as a car presenter?"

"Well, only from the last motor show at Beijing."

"Great. Folks tell me that you are pretty good at it."

"Well, thank you sir for noticing. In fact it's just a temporary assignment; I have a job as a customer service executive at the largest multi-brand car showroom in Mumbai."

"Oh, I see, that's really nice."

"You know I go personally into some of our exclusive dealership outlets to talk to our customer service executives, because they are the ones who handle the customers. But it's so many of them we can't possibly do that for them all, it's quite difficult getting vital feedbacks directly to customers."

"I can understand sir."

"So how do you feel handling the customers?"

"I love it. I'm always busy handling the angry ones."

"Really?"

"That's because when they turn up, all my colleagues just pass them on to me."

"I see. And how do you manage them? We have been consistently trying to invest in refining our products but we're not as fast."

"Sir, you will be surprised to know that most times the customers are angry about problems in the car that have simple solutions, only they don't have enough information and cannot seem to understand the manuals."

"You are right Parth, we have noticed too."

"And when they come in, no one wants to deal with the angry ones."

"You know Parth, it's an interesting fact."

"We need to solve this problem. Do you have an idea in mind? We need to keep giving people good services."

Parth could sense the opportunity. The words "need" started flowing through his mind as he remembered one of the conversations he had with Prabhudas on financial understanding.

"You add value when you solve basic needs or meet people's interests."

"I have found out that most of the complaints that customers come in with are not well covered in the brochures and manuals, hence the staff at car showrooms do not have enough knowledge to give simple solutions that exist. In many cases across showrooms, they also have their sales targets so they always want to get on with new customers so that no one wants to handle post-sales customers that much."

"So what do you suggest?"

"What if we set up kiosks at car dealerships with regularly updated video manuals on the frequently faced problems for the angry customers? I'd say one in every ten of our customers will find it useful. Also these days everyone can search videos on the internet and stream them on their mobile phones. So you will have less angry customers."

"That's an amazing idea and we would love to implement that right away. We know once we start, other manufacturers will adopt same."

"Are you open to work with us on a flexible payment system? You help us with the creation of such FAQ videos for your region and see how customers respond. We will pay you say $2 per uniquely verified views on videos seen across kiosks and on all personal digital devices for the first year."

"$2 per customer? How many views do you expect?"

"Well we usually get about 500,000 uniquely verified views every year. But who knows with your popularity, who says we couldn't have more?"

Parth's heart skipped briefly. This was a possibility of $1 million staring him in the face.

"That's about a million dollars at the end of the year?"

"Yes, quite conveniently."

As Parth was walking back to his hotel, he couldn't stop crying. All he remembered was conversations with Prabhudas. Parth couldn't believe how the times had turned around for him so radically after meeting Prabhudas. It had been six hard months though earning just 8,000 rupees and he and his family suffered.

His dad and mum had come under the same pressure as when he was still an undergraduate. But at this point, since they didn't know how long this episode will last, they had to come up with a more sustainable plan. They couldn't squeeze themselves perpetually.

His dad joined a cooperative society to help raise some capital to boost his mother's trade, as she got some new and very skilled employees to help improve her sales. She couldn't do more than the number of work days the doctors prescribed for her, but this new move helped. His dad also got into some form of trade programmes organized by the government and farmers of cash crops. The income they both got wasn't so much, but it filled the gap. It had broken his heart to see them work that hard again, and it had been why he got restless about his financial progress.

Now he wanted to compensate them.

"In one year from now, I will get my first $1 million dollar pay check" he said out loud in the bathroom as the steamy water warmly washed off the sweat and dirt of the day.

He called home to break the news.

"Krisha it has happened!" He was excited as he also broke the news to Krisha after speaking with his family.

*   *   *

Four years Later...

After being with *"The Concept Motors & Showroom"* for a little over four *years*, Parth felt that it was time for him to move on. He could feel it, but had not yet figured out how to go about it. He and Krisha had now been married for three years and she had given birth to a son whom they named *Prabhudas*. The name sounded a bit old fashioned for the new generation. But both Parth and Krisha felt their son could be a trendsetter with it when the rest of the kids' names are too modern. Krisha had also just been honoured by the government with a national award for her role in promoting the arts. Though Krisha had been talking about how Kolpur was strategic to her goals in divesting the activities of the gallery in the local market from the international market, but their lives seemed at that moment to be better suited in Mumbai.

"Sweetheart, I have been thinking for a while about opening my own dealership and Kolpur is looking to me like a perfect place to do that. You know since you started talking about Kolpur, we couldn't really see ourselves moving there and stopping our life here. But Kolpur is growing fast these days, don't you think it's time we opened this new chapter?" Parth asked.

"My love, I agree with you. I think I have lost my fears of starting in an unfamiliar town. Somehow I have unconsciously fallen in love with the place, but I was thinking of the best time to broach the topic with you. I am glad you are thinking of owning your own place, you seem to have outgrown *The Concept Motors*".

Parth had entered into several deals with many brands after the deal with BMZ Cars, especially because he needed to look neutral. *The Concept*

Motors had become really successful and a household name. It was time for him to move on. He had enough money now to enter into a dealership, he needed to keep growing.

Ashutosh and the other staff were very emotional during the farewell lunch where Ashutosh announced Parth's departure. They shared wonderful memories and had a great time.

"We will be seeing Parth around sometimes. So don't get too emotional. He remains as my business partner and I'll make sure to bring him to our showroom." Ashutosh mentioned at the farewell

Krisha on her part found it really difficult parting with her staff—they shed tears and very emotional moments. She entered into a joint venture with a management company that would help retain the world class nature of the Mumbai gallery, while she would visit occasionally but mainly supervise the collections and art pieces from Kolpur.

She now mass produced popular artworks that were voted by locals during the local exhibitions, and the pieces sold quite fast, while the original copies sold for much more. Some artistes preferred to do only the exclusives and not mass produce, though their pieces were more expensive, but it didn't move as fast as the mass produced ones. Sometimes mass production also meant more money.

Parth and Krisha were two individuals who had been through rough experiences but were finding new chapters opening out in their lives with new meaning and a sense of fulfillment.

*   *   *

The opening of the *"New Gate Motors & Showroom"* was a grand day. Parth, his immediate and extended family and close friends gathered in the fast growing town of Kolpur where Parth's own multi-brand car dealership was being opened. The facility was spread over a massive area just as *the concept car showroom* in Mumbai.

It had been four years since Parth had the meeting with BMZ's MD, and Parth's customer service videos were now serving over 300 car dealerships in the world.

As Parth stood with Krisha and their son in front of the showroom on the morning of its inauguration, tears kept flowing from his eyes. Krisha wrapped her left hand around him.

"I wish Prabhudas could be here Krisha. He would have been so happy."

"I believe he is honey. Remember he said he would always be around. I can feel him."

Parth was wondering how the small seed of love had transformed into the grand success it had become almost effortlessly. He had worked really hard, but it had been an enjoyable ride all the way.

Parth went back into memories with Prabhudas, his attraction to Ashwini, the confusion and suffocation he had felt for years, and the thoughts of committing suicide after he lost his job and got his heart broken.

It was Prabhudas' conversations that had also given Parth the patience to find his true love in his beloved Krisha whom he truly loved with all his soul—a beautiful and exceptional woman in every sense of the word, who had captured his heart and had showered him with so much love.

Parth's parents were now with him. Parth's father came forward to him and said "Son, I must have done some good work for god to have given me a son like you. God has indeed blessed us."

They all laughed and went to meet the other guests as they checked out the cars.

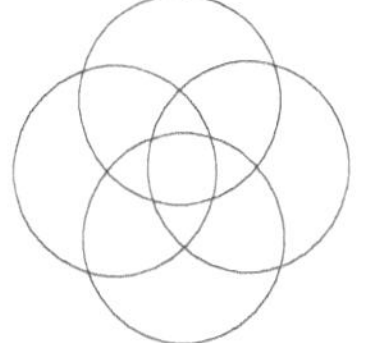

Chapter Fourteen—Epilogue

Parth's story is one that truly captures the struggles that many youths face in their late teens and early twenties. For some, it extends much longer, throwing up even more difficult situations and depressing challenges. Yet, the power that every youth has at this strategic time is infinite, but most find themselves directionless and lost. In extreme cases, some actually commit suicide, while many others narrowly escape from such thoughts and plans. The challenges of life aren't worth you taking your life, what you need is the right perception to those realities.

We realize that there are important elements of youth life that hold it together, such as faith, family, career and love life. Success in the love life and career of a youth for instance emerges from a fundamental understanding of the human heart. Beyond the biological connotations, the heart has a wide meaning for everyone.

Sometimes it gets really difficult to separate things happening in the deepest recesses of our hearts from the noise that is projected all around us—we get lost in the noise and become agitated or disillusioned. Those who succeed in life usually have a clear sense of direction and a somewhat keen sense of purpose. But when we all get up in the morning, the brief tranquility of the morning soon gives way to the distractions of the day—and this could go on for years. We are surrounded daily by the social, academic, family, financial, political and other forms of disturbing headlines in the media and distracting discussions in our daily activities. Soon because of the superficial noise, people forget to discover who they really are.

The principles of *Ikigai* shared in this book, are known to have really changed the lives of many people. It is not exclusive to the Japanese. Many experts have adopted the Japanese name because it has been promoted in that culture as a unique concept. Read closely the captivating dialogues captured in this story of a young man who went from being rejected at work and in the game of love, to finding true success in an unlikely career, and falling in love with a woman who herself had failed at love twice. The nuggets in the story and its compelling literary beauty could change your life forever—for real. It should also whet your appetite to embark on your own journey to discovering more about *Ikigai* and its cogent principles for successful living.

References:

The readings that inspired me to write this content:

"Ikigai: The Japanese secret to a long and happy life"- Héctor García , Francesc Miralles

"The Seven Spiritual Laws of Success" - Deepak Chopra

"The Secret" - Rhonda Byrne

"Rich Dad Poor Dad" - Robert Kiyosaki

"The Toyota way" - LIKER and JEFFREY

About the Author :

Atul Khekade (In my own words)

I'm a first generation entrepreneur in Banking, Fintech, Crypto domain. I'm the Co-Founder of XinFin (exchange infinite) or XDC Network, a blockchain crypto coin based platform aimed at helping over 450 Million MSMEs get access to capital for growth. The platform is built on the foundation of Decentralised Finance or DeFi. The MSMEs employ nearly half of the world's population.

As a serial entrepreneur, I have built a global distribution system for Air Charter Industry and an executive education platform. I've led a startup to build a fraud prevention system in the Banking and Finance industry.

In the years to come, I plan to work close to the grassroots level to ensure Fintech/Blockchain based banking reaches every person in the world enabling financial freedom.

How to Reach me :

Email : atulpkhekade@gmail.com

Twitter : @atulkhekade

Linkedin : https://www.linkedin.com/in/atul-khekade-9076b36